AUTHOR	CLASS
MORICE, A	BL F R

TITLE   Treble exposure

Treble Exposure

Lorraine Thurloe, a close friend of Tessa Crichton, is shortly to arrive in England as a member of a group of American whodunnit addicts on a 'Mystery Tour'.

With her are the daughters of a lately-widowed friend, one of whom, Beverly, has only recently left a nursing home where she had been treated for manic depression. Her doctors now think a change of environment would further aid her recovery.

Tessa isn't so sure, particularly when a woman is found murdered on Roakes Common a few hours after Beverly has been there. Beverly also confesses to seeing ghosts and her family and friends begin to believe her 'progress' is leading her straight back to an institution.

Naturally, Tessa is intrigued by both the mystery and the young girl's behaviour, so spends a lot more time with Lorraine and the tour than she would otherwise have done. With her usual erratic intuitiveness, Tessa unravels the complex relationships and motives which led to the murder, but another death is to occur before she can expose the killer.

Anne Morice is held in affectionate esteem for her light-hearted but satisfying mysteries. *Treble Exposure* is another delightful example of her talents.

by the same author

DEATH IN THE GRAND MANOR
MURDER IN MARRIED LIFE
DEATH OF A GAY DOG
MURDER ON FRENCH LEAVE
DEATH AND THE DUTIFUL DAUGHTER
DEATH OF A HEAVENLY TWIN
KILLING WITH KINDNESS
NURSERY TEA AND POISON
DEATH OF A WEDDING GUEST
MURDER IN MIMICRY
SACRED TO DEATH
MURDER BY PROXY
MURDER IN OUTLINE
DEATH IN THE ROUND
THE MEN IN HER DEATH
HOLLOW VENGEANCE
SLEEP OF DEATH
MURDER POST-DATED
GETTING AWAY WITH MURDER?
DEAD ON CUE
PUBLISH AND BE KILLED

Anne Morice
TREBLE EXPOSURE

MACMILLAN
LONDON

First published in the UK 1987 by
MACMILLAN LONDON LIMITED
4 Little Essex Street London WC2R 3LF
and Basingstoke

Associated companies in Auckland, Delhi, Dublin, Gaborone,
Hamburg, Harare, Hong Kong, Johannesburg, Kuala Lumpur,
Lagos, Manzini, Melbourne, Mexico City, Nairobi, New York,
Singapore and Tokyo

British Library Cataloguing in Publication Data

Morice, Anne
    Treble exposure.   02711489
    I. Title
    823'.914 [F]   PR6063.0743

ISBN 0-333-44967-3

Typeset in Times by Bookworm Typesetting, Salford

Printed and bound in the UK by Anchor Brendon Ltd, Essex

1

I tend to think of my friend, Lorraine Thurloe, as a catalyst. It is not a word I often use, having something to do with chemical reactions, I understand, but it bobs up from time to time in scripts and it has just the right ring about it for Lorraine.

She might also be described as a thunderbolt, harmless in itself but liable to leave a chain of catastrophes in its wake. Furthermore, being American, her bolts tend to be on a larger and more thunderous scale than those nearer home and her wake correspondingly more extensive.

For this reason, and dearly as I love her, I react with a certain wariness at the sight of her handwriting on an envelope – especially one which is adorned with about four dollars' worth of postage stamps – such as I received from her one Monday morning towards the end of last May.

I read it on the train going up to Oxford, the post having arrived half an hour before my departure from Beacon Square, when every particle of concentration was required for last-minute instructions for Mrs Cheeseman, in the atmosphere of mounting tension which always overtakes Robin when either of us has a train to catch.

Leaving my car behind had been something of a wrench, but after careful deliberation I had decided that it would only be a liability during my three-week sojourn in Oxford. All those colleges cluttering up the place make it virtually impossible to find a parking space and Robin had promised to give it a reassuring pat and to keep it tuned up to a lively pitch in such odd moments as he could spare from the demands of life as a

5

Detective Chief Inspector at Scotland Yard.

'The only trouble is,' he had objected, 'I thought we were both spending next weekend with your cousin Toby at Roakes Common.'

'Yes, we are.'

'So how will you get there without a car?'

'Oh, cadge a lift, I suppose. There's bound to be someone in the company who's going to London for the weekend and Roakes is practically on the way.'

'And how will they overcome the parking problem?'

'By leaving their cars in the vaults of the hotel, I daresay, there to remain, clocking up parking fees till the end of the run. That's their worry and they must work it out for themselves.'

Faith in the wisdom of my decision to travel by train got a major boost from the fact that we had whizzed through the first half of the journey and were already pulling out of Reading by the time I reached the end of Lorraine's letter.

It began with the news of her impending visit to England, followed by endearing expressions of her enchantment at the prospect of seeing Robin and me again and then by the announcement that I would never believe this, but she would not be on her own, or even with Henry, but in the company of eleven other people, all but three of whom she had yet to meet. They were members of an ultra-select package tour, which some enterprising travel agency had laid on to cater specifically for mystery-story addicts. The object was to traipse with reverential footsteps around the haunts of such well-known characters as Lord Peter Wimsey, Hercule Poirot, Sherlock Holmes and a number of others whose names she could not for the moment recall, but felt sure I would recognise if I heard them.

It was quite hard to believe, as it happened, because, although she was an avid reader and whipped through every new novel and biography which Henry courteously ordered for her once a month from Brentanos, I had never, when the parcel was unpacked, seen more than an occasional crime story or thriller come tumbling out. With the sensation, however, that I was now reading one myself, I hurried on to paragraph one, page three.

'Remember Lynn Finkelstein?' it began. 'Henry and I took you to visit her and Earl and their two daughters at their place in Conn. one weekend when you were last over (which is far too long, almost a year, by the way). Earl died soon after that. Collapsed with a heart attack at Virginia and Ed's wedding and only lived a few days. Virginia's the elder girl, the other one's called Beverly, and at one time we all thought she was the one Ed had his eye on. Wrong, though, because he married Virginia and it was one great big, splashy wedding with about a thousand guests, foie gras flown in from France, along with the bridesmaids' dresses and a couple of symphony orchestras thrown in.

'It turned out to be their last extravagance, though, and Lynn's been having a rough time ever since. First of all, the shock and then discovering Earl had spent practically every cent he made and, on top of that, there was Beverly's problem, which was the worst horror of all. She was just into her second year at college at this time and Lynn was going out of her mind, wondering how she could afford to keep her there for the full course. She didn't need to lose any sleep over that side of it, though, because it was about then that Bev started acting so strange. Up to then, she'd always been a good-natured, simple sort of girl, not a bit like her sister, but almost overnight there was this transformation. She stopped turning up for classes, which meant her marks took a plunge and that led to fits of depression and she just seemed incapable of pulling herself out of the spiral. At first, everyone was inclined to let it ride. They thought it was all on account of Earl's death, but then it got so bad they called in the shrink and he diagnosed it as advanced manic depression and shot her into this hell-hole of a clinic, where they pumped her full of drugs which just seemed to make her ten times worse, and they said it might be years before they could get the treatment really right. Can you imagine? Poor

Lynn, it was as much as she could do to pay the expenses of going up there to visit her, let alone finding the hospital fees.

'The climax finally came when Beverly got involved in some brawl with one of the nurses. I never heard the details, but there was one hell of a hullaballoo. The nurse accused Beverly of having tried to throttle her and for a while the poor child was kept under guard in a padded cell.

'That was when Henry persuaded Lynn to let him take over. She'd always flatly refused to accept financial help for herself, but since it was one of the girls she did manage to swallow her pride, on the understanding she'd pay back every cent just as soon as she got on her feet again, which, as you can imagine, was about the last thing to bother Henry.

'Anyway, after a month or two everything did begin to look up. Henry had a hand in that too, I guess, because the first thing he did was to get Bev moved into Bella Vista, which is a really gorgeous place in up-state NY, more like some luxurious country mansion than a sanitarium, in beautiful surroundings and all the doctors and nursing staff friendly and relaxed. The best thing of all was that it meant only a forty-mile drive for Lynn so she was able to visit several times a week, which did them both good, and from then on Bev hasn't really looked back. There was a trial period when she was allowed home for weekends and when that worked out OK they said she could live at home and just go to Bella Vista three mornings a week for what they call instructional therapy classes. That worked well, too, and about a month ago the head psychiatrist said she was ready to stand on her own two feet and what he recommended now was a change of environment. She had to put the bad times behind her and make a fresh start. He's a wonderful man, incidentally, and it wouldn't surprise me if he was motivated partly by the idea that this was what Lynn needed too.

'OK, Tessa, I can just hear you thinking: "Lord, how Lorraine does go on!", which I don't for one minute deny, but I'm nearly there now and the end is where you come into the

8

story. At least, I'm hoping it is (and so is Henry, which is sure to melt your resistance). Trouble was, you see, that getting Beverly fixed up with somewhere to go for this change of environment wasn't all that easy. She couldn't just go drifting off on her own, she'd need supervision and it would have to come from someone tolerant and understanding. The only one who seemed right for that job was Lynn herself, which wouldn't have been much of a solution. In the end it was Ed, of all people, who came up with the answer. He'd read this advertisement for the High and Wide Travel Bureau, who were setting up a very exclusive package tour for mystery readers, and it started some bells ringing in that beautiful head of his. He remembered how during Beverly's last few weeks at Bella Vista she had taken to spending a lot of time in the library. It was mostly light stuff she was going for, romance and suspense stories, that kind of thing, and the doctors took it as a good sign. They liked it better than ever when she invented some elaborate treasure- murder-hunt game for the staff and patients, with clues strewn around over the house and grounds. She really worked hard on it and they had a lot of fun, so it gave her a great confidence boost. Ed said this was the answer they'd been looking for and he talked Virginia into giving up their trip to Italy this summer and taking Bev on the Mystery Tour instead.

'One of the scheduled stop-over places is Oxford, where they're due to spend two or three days, going on walks round some of the colleges that figure in those books, taking photographs of each other standing on the exact spot where Lord Peter proposed to whoever it was, and this is where you have an important role. I remember you told me that you were doing this play in Oxford just about the time we'll be there, which clinched it as far as I was concerned, and I have decided to become a mystery addict myself for those three weeks. How's that for a new departure?

'Henry's all for it. Normally, he hates me to go abroad without him, but he sees this as a real constructive good deed, with maybe quite a lot of fun thrown in. What he means is, I guess, that it will give Virginia a feeling of security to have someone older – if not wiser – along. Like, if Beverly should have some kind of relapse, there'd be someone to turn to. If so, he probably flatters me, but then when didn't he? Which reminds me, I'm going to be forty, for the very first time, next birthday, so perhaps this is a good moment to start learning how to become a chaperone.

'Anyway, it's all fixed and our party flies out from Kennedy on the 20th (almost as soon as you're likely to be reading this) and their eyes will pop when I tell them – and I'm certainly going to tell them – that they'll have a chance to meet the celebrated Theresa Crichton and, furthermore, that her husband is (or very soon will be) Deputy Head of Scotland Yard. We'll be staying in London from Saturday morning through Monday, at the New Westminster Hotel. As I see it, that must be good news too, because with a name like that how could it be more than a block or two away from your house on Beacon Square?

'Could you call me there some time late Saturday afternoon? We're to see some Agatha Christie play in the evening, so make it before six, if you can, and let me know whether you're still around, or in Oxford, or wherever.

'Monday is a tight schedule, with an expedition to Baker Street in search of that famous apartment, sitting in at some trial at the Old Bailey and exciting things like that (Chamber of Horrors, for all I know), but I don't intend being completely tied down and could pull out of part of the program, if you're going to be around. And Sunday is a kind of rest day, when we're on our own and can do what we want. What I want most is to see you and Robin, so do your best for me. Henry sends oceans of love and so do I, Lorraine.'

When I had finished unpacking there was just time left for two urgent jobs on the domestic front. The first was to telephone Mrs Cheeseman with a list of all the things I had left behind, so that she could pack them up for Robin to bring down to Roakes at the weekend. That done, I moved on to her counterpart in my cousin Toby's household at Roakes Common, who is also the gardener's wife and is called Mrs Parkes.

She answered the telephone in person and, after a few polite preliminaries back and forth, I requested her to apprise her employer of the likelihood of there being one, and possibly as many as four, extra guests for Sunday luncheon. Some people might have seen this as a back-to-front way of going about it, but, with only ten minutes left before I was due at the theatre, it was by far the most practical.

In no circumstances does Toby answer the telephone himself and he can rarely be persuaded to speak into it, except in direst emergency. Furthermore, had I by some miracle or oversight succeeded in establishing contact, he would probably have forgotten all about the extra numbers for lunch within five minutes of putting the receiver down; whereas to Mrs Parkes it was a matter of some moment, as she demonstrated by saying:

'Well, thanks for letting me know. I'd had it in mind to order a fillet of beef for Sunday, when it was just going to be you and the Inspector, but we couldn't very well stretch that to six or seven, could we? I'll have to think again. Anything particular you fancy?'

'Absolutely everything, Mrs Parkes, you know me! But Mrs Thurloe will be among the party, so spare no effort.'

'Oh, that's nice,' Mrs Parkes replied primly, no doubt reminded of the handsome leather bag with which Lorraine had presented her on her last visit to Roakes Common.

11

2

In the event, only Lorraine and Beverly turned up and Robin telephoned to say he could not get down till the evening, so the fillet would have stretched, after all. Still, there's a lot to be said for roast sirloin and Yorkshire pudding, although it has to be admitted that neither guest seemed specially eager to say it. Lorraine cut up everything like a good girl, then swished it all round her plate like a bad one, while Beverly incurred Mrs Parkes's silent displeasure by asking for second helpings of everything, without troubling herself to finish the first, and Toby's by preferring tomato juice to wine.

They had arrived earlier than expected in a powerful-looking hired car, Lorraine having explained to me in advance that this arrangement would give Ed and Virginia the chance to go off somewhere on their own for a few hours, before they were sucked into three solid weeks of group activity. She had looked rather wan on arrival, but I had attributed this to a combination of jet lag and the fact that she was missing Henry, from whom she had scarcely been parted since their marriage five years before. However, as lunch proceeded I began to wonder if it was not simply the over-exuberance of her companion which made her, by contrast, appear more subdued than usual.

A table and four chairs had been set out on the back verandah for our coffee, but Beverly neglected hers in order to prance around and click away with her camera, which was worn on a gold chain around her neck. She appeared to be a somewhat indiscriminate photographer, though, close-ups of the coffee pot being treated with as much care as panoramic views of the house, and at one point she went down on her knees to train the camera on a poppy bud. All this, she explained to us, was to enable her to recreate the atmosphere for posterity, though it was hard to follow the reasoning behind this, one poppy being so much like another.

'Still a shade on the manic side, would you say?' I suggested when she had left us to explore the beautiful, beautiful garden.

'Perhaps I'm wrong, though,' I added, as Lorraine remained silent and glum, fiddling with a loose strand of binding on the arm of her chair and looking as though nothing in the world mattered so much to her as getting it back into its right pattern. 'Perhaps she is simply a natural extrovert and all this excitability simply indicates that she's back to normal?'

'What depresses me,' Toby said, 'is how banal I can be in my instant judgements. All those carroty curls, flouncy skirts and freckles would have fooled me completely. The perfect Anne of Green Gables stereotype and the last girl on earth I would have associated with nervous breakdowns and psychiatrists. It is a sad admission for one who passes himself off as a professional playwright.'

'You wouldn't have been far out, at that,' Lorraine told him, 'she is a bit like that, always has been. What worries me is how badly she's starting to overdo it. Imagine all that dancing around and squealing. Any minute, I was afraid she would clap her hands and say she was off to look for the Teddy Bears' Picnic.'

'She could well have found it, too,' Toby remarked sourly. 'The most unspeakable people park their cars and bring out their sausage rolls and Coca Cola as near to our boundary as they can get on Sunday mornings at this time of year.'

'Do they really?' Lorraine asked, looking startled. 'I hadn't noticed.'

'You should know by now that you have to allow for a little exaggeration,' I reminded her. 'There was one historic occasion a year or two ago when no less than two cars were parked on the Common. It was contravening all the rules of the Doomsday Book, I need hardly say, and they were seen off, but ever since then Toby has been comparing the place unfavourably with Coney Island in mid-August. Perhaps he is partly to blame,' I added, 'for Beverly overdoing her act. All his wild talk and disparagement of things most people hold sacred is making her feel nervous and insecure.'

'Oh no, Tessa, none of it's Toby's fault this time. The mood was getting a hold on her long before we arrived here. You ought to have seen the way she drove that car down the freeway.'

'Which way was that?'

'As though she had the wind behind her and no other car on the road. She was like someone who'd been drinking champagne for the first time in her life. Or had fallen in love for the first time. Neither of which seems very likely.'

'Perhaps it was a mistake to hire such a powerful car?'

'Oh, sure, I can see that now, Tessa, but I'd left all that side of it to her, you see. When I told her we'd been invited to spend the day here, she was all for it, and she offered to arrange everything with the hall porter, so I let her go ahead. Since she was going to be the one to drive, that seemed logical.'

'Oh, indeed, but why was she? You're a marvellous driver and you know your way around in this country as well as I do. I'd have said the logical choice would be you.'

'And you're probably right, but the way I saw it was this: she's come on so well these last few months, really almost back to her old style, and I thought it would be another step forward for her to feel ... well ... trustworthy and responsible.'

'It seems to have had rather the opposite effect.'

'Oh, don't you start on me, Toby! I feel bad enough as it is and I could kick myself. Who the hell do I think I am to set myself up as some goddam analyst? We were warned that she'd need supervision and my function was to provide it, not try out my own little amateur theories. Far as I can see, all I've done is set her back a few miles. If Henry ever gets to hear about it, he'll probably have me bundled off to Bella Vista myself and I wouldn't blame him.'

14

'Oh, come on, now, Lorraine, no need to make such a tragedy of it. You both got here in one piece and when you leave you must make sure it's you in the driving seat.'

'What if Beverly has other ideas?'

'Ignore them. You've tried treating her as trustworthy and responsible and it didn't work, so now you must play it the other way. Tell her there'll be a lot of traffic going back into London on Sunday evening, which is true, and that, unlike her, you're experienced in the local customs, so that's that.'

'Well, yes, I guess you're right, Tessa.'

'And cheer up! Things are bound to improve when the tour proper gets under way tomorrow. What you've overlooked is that she's become accustomed to being herded about and told how to fill every minute of her day. She'll feel quite at home once that courier has rounded you all up and taken control.'

'So what the hell am I doing, letting her wander off on her own now? And how long has she been gone? Twenty minutes, half an hour? God Almighty, the yard's not that vast.'

'No need to be insulting,' Toby said. 'And she's not far away. I saw her a moment or two ago, flitting about among those vulgar cypress trees which Parkes insisted on planting, to screen the garage. And here she comes, you see,' he added a moment or two later, 'or have we now moved to Elsinore?'

The question was not inept because, as Beverly advanced towards us, we saw that a rather worrying change had come about, transforming Anne of Green Gables into a cross between Ophelia and a somewhat beleaguered Gypsy Lass. Her hair was tangled and had a collection of leaves stuck to it, part of the flouncy hem had come unstitched and she was barefooted. She carried her shoes in one hand and, in the other, a bunch of wilting dandelions, which she tossed into Toby's lap before flopping down on the grass, hunching her knees and wrapping her arms around them.

It was a tribute to Lorraine and incontrovertible evidence of his deep affection for her that Toby did not then mutter something about having a difficult scene to deal with in the play

15

he was working on and disappear into the house for the rest of the afternoon. Instead he said mildly, having transferred the flowers to the table:

'How pretty! We must ask Mrs Parkes to put them in water until you go back to London.'

'I picked them for you,' Beverly said in a mournful voice.

'Most kind, but I wouldn't dream of depriving you. We have more than we need in the garden.'

I noticed, or fancied I did, a flash of genuine amusement in Beverly's eyes, but it came and went in under a second. It occurred to me then to ask myself whether she might not be playing at being dotty and, if so, whether that might be more or less dangerous form of dottiness than the straightforward one.

'Come on!' Toby said, easing himself out of his reclining chair, as well as metaphorically rising to still greater heights of tolerance. 'Just time for a game of croquet before tea, I should say. You and Beverly can take on Lorraine and me, Tessa.'

'But I don't know how to play croquet,' Beverly wailed, looking terrified.

'You'll soon pick it up,' I assured her. 'I'll explain the rules as we go along and the first one is to put your shoes back on. One false move with the mallet and you could find yourself with eight broken toes.'

I was about to add that it would also be advisable to remove the camera from around her neck, but then saw that she had already done so.

Toby marched ahead, with Beverly trotting along behind and Lorraine and me following at a more leisurely pace.

'I don't suppose you'd consider breaking that Oxford contract, would you, Tess?'

'No, I'm sure I wouldn't. What an extraordinary idea!'

'Yes, I know, but I just thought it would be nice to have you along on the tour with us,' she explained. 'Something tells me we may be going to need you.'

3

Robin turned up an hour or two after the others had left and we were still exchanging news and views of the day's events when the telephone rang.

Toby never touches it himself, if it can be avoided and keeps it hidden in the most inconvenient place he can think of, so I had to leave the cosy scene and go out to the hall to answer it. It was Lorraine, calling to report on their safe arrival in London, with no emotional or mechanical hitches on the way.

'Good! Beverly has calmed down, in other words?'

'To be frank with you, Tessa, I wouldn't be too sure of that. She was very quiet on the way back, kind of subdued, but I didn't let it bother me. I put it down to her being tired and why not, for God's sake? It's not everyone who has to go through the ordeal of playing croquet with Toby on their first day in Europe. Who wouldn't be tired?'

'Who, indeed. I am myself.'

'Well, yes, but then, just as we were coming into the city and I was concentrating on trying to figure out which lane we ought to aim for on the Cromwell Road, she said something strange. Do you want me to tell you what she said?'

'Why not?'

'She asked me if I believed in ghosts.'

'Oh well, not very brilliant timing, perhaps, but not particularly startling or unusual. It's a question that often seems to crop up for no special reason. What did you answer?'

'I said I believed in keeping an open mind on the subject, but I'd never seen one myself and, until I did, I took the attitude that when you were dead you were dead and that was it. So then what do you think she said?'

'Can't imagine.'

'She said she hadn't been talking about dead people. What she'd meant was, would it be possible for someone who was still alive to have a ghost? I was a bit fazed, but I tried to act kind of jokey and I asked her whether this one was walking around with its head under its arm and, you're never going to believe this, Tessa, but she said in a sort of deadpan voice, "No, it was putting some luggage into the trunk of a car." What would your reaction have been to that?'

'I'll tell you exactly what my reaction would have been, Lorraine. That I think it's time you stopped watching her and weighing every word she utters. Lots of girls of her age fantasise and come out with other-worldly remarks of that nature, from time to time, either to get attention, or because they like to see themselves as more spiritual and sensitive than all us philistines and cynics. It's not necessarily a sign of insanity and you wouldn't have given it a second thought if you hadn't known her history and background.'

There was a pause at the other end of the line and then Lorraine said, 'You know something, Tessa? I think you may have a point there. I never saw it that way before and I bet Virginia hasn't either. It certainly is something to remember and I'm grateful to you for pointing it out.'

'You're welcome,' I said, trying out my American accent. 'And good luck on the rest of the trip. See you in Oxford.'

'Where's Robin?' I asked on my return to the parlour.

'Conferring in the kitchen with Mrs Parkes.'

'What about?'

'I have no idea. She came in here when the telephone rang, wearing her well-known mask of suppressed excitement, to ask if she might have a private word with the Inspector, so it would appear to be a matter of some gravity.'

'Perhaps she wants to find out how she would stand with the

18

law if she were to lace your soup with arsenic, in revenge for being instructed to stand the dandelions in iced water.'

'Yes, most likely.'

Robin re-entered the room at this point, putting an end to speculation. He was looking grave, but it appeared that the crisis did not directly concern any member of the household.

'There seems to have been a nasty incident on the Common this afternoon,' he announced.

'I am sure there was,' Toby replied. 'Have you ever known a Sunday go by without one? What was it this time? One of those picnicking parties gone hurtling back to London, leaving the cat to fend for itself?'

'Worse, I'm afraid. This time they seem to have left one of their number behind and in no fit state to fend for herself, I have to tell you.'

'Do stop being enigmatic, Robin. It doesn't become you, and Tessa and I are feeling far too whacked for riddles.'

'Very well, in plain words, about an hour ago a woman was found dead in the copse across the road from the Common.'

'Really? Found by whom?'

'A pair of your infamous picnickers. Mrs Parkes doesn't know their names or anything about them. The copse is choked with brambles and undergrowth, as you probably know, and it's her view that they had gone there seeing it as a handy place to dump all the litter they didn't want to take home. However, she's almost as jaundiced as you are about the Sunday invaders and, anyway, that's beside the point.'

'How was she killed?'

'Strangled, I gather, with her own silk scarf, although the last bit may have been thrown in to lend colour. As you may imagine, there are no end of rumours flying around.'

'So what did these people do, having made their disagreeable discovery?'

'One of them went to the telephone outside the pub to call an ambulance and the other, who'd had some training in first aid, stayed behind to try a little artificial respiration, in case she was still alive. If she had been, it would most likely have finished her off, but that's also beside the point.'

'And all this happened only an hour or two ago, you say? I don't remember hearing any commotion.'

'Well, you wouldn't, would you, Toby? Not for nothing have you spent all these years perfecting the art of switching off your eyes and ears to anything that goes on beyond your own boundaries.'

Up till then I had taken no part in the discussion, since they seemed to be managing quite well without me, but Toby's last remark had revived a memory.

'I did, though,' I told them. 'Well, perhaps you couldn't exactly call it a commotion, more of a gentle stir. It was towards the end of the game, when Beverly gave her ball such a mighty whack that it went about forty yards beyond the post. I took her over there and started to explain the rules about getting it back into the game, but after a moment or two I realised she wasn't listening. She was staring past me, out over the Common, and that's when I saw it.'

'Saw what?' Robin asked in the patient voice he no doubt reserved for more garrulous witnesses.

'There was quite a crowd of people grouped around in an aimless sort of way on the far side of the Common, by the road. There were several cars parked on the road too, although it's so narrow just there, and in front of them a big white van with a flashing light on top. I thought it must be an ice-cream van and I warned Beverly not to breathe a word about it to Toby, otherwise he'd have twenty heart attacks in quick succession. Of course, I realise now that it must have been an ambulance.'

'I'm thankful you didn't tell me,' Toby said. 'An ambulance would have been quite bad enough. Who was this woman, by the way, Robin? Not anyone we know, presumably, otherwise you would have told us already.'

'I can't say whether you knew her or not. Mrs Parkes hasn't yet been able to find out her name, but she wasn't a local, as far as anyone knows.'

'Well, that's good and I really don't see any need for us to concern ourselves with it. I feel sorry for her, naturally, and sorrier still that it should have happened here, but I cannot imagine why Mrs Parkes has to make such a mystery of it. I am not so hysterical and sensitive as all that, am I?'

'No, but I think she's afraid you may be drawn in, whether you like it or not, and she wanted to test my reactions to that possibility.'

'What rubbish! How could we be drawn in? So far as we're aware, none of us knows the first thing about the wretched woman and, if it's eyewitnesses they want, we should be worse than useless. As Tessa has just told you, we were heavily engaged in more important matters while this fracas was going on.'

'When she was found, you mean? She could have been attacked some considerable time before that. An hour, possibly two or three.'

'It amounts to the same thing. We were either indoors, having lunch, or sitting on the verandah at the back.'

'Are you certain that applies to all of you?'

'Certainly I am.'

'But Tessa had also told me, before we heard about this, that at one point Beverly went tripping off on her own.'

'Quite so. She wished to explore the garden, but she was flitting about in full view of the rest of us most of the time.'

'You can vouch for that, can you?'

'My dear Robin, is this an official interrogation, or just curiosity on your part?'

'Neither. I am simply trying to give you a foretaste of what Mrs Parkes is afraid may lie ahead.'

'Oh, the hell with Mrs Parkes. What's it got to do with her, anyway?'

'I'll tell you exactly what. She maintains, rightly in my opinion, that if it could ever be proved that Parkes had all those dandelions blooming and flourishing among his precious lawns and beds, you would sack him on the spot. Always assuming, of course, that he had not already committed suicide.'

21

4

It was nearly ten o'clock by the time Robin left. He had offered to drive me over to Oxford before going on to London, but it would have added forty miles to his journey and he had an early start in the morning, so I told him I proposed to spend another night at Roakes. I did not have to report for work until 10.00 a.m. and would either prevail upon Toby to take me, or to allow Mr Parkes to act as chauffeur.

After seeing him off, I toyed with the idea of putting a call through to the New Westminster Hotel but, on reflection, decided to postpone that until the morning too. Knowing Lorraine of old, I realised that she would be most unlikely to retire to her room much before midnight and, as she is liable to say whatever comes into her head regardless of her surroundings, or who might overhear, it was essential to ensure that her end of the conversation, at least, should be conducted in private.

It turned out to be the right decision because, by a strange coincidence, someone else evidently had similar views about Toby's bedtime routine and a few moments later we had a caller. I noticed, on going into the hall to let him in, that I had left the front door partly open after Robin's departure and it would have been a far greater misfortune if any part of my end of the conversation with Lorraine had been overheard by this of all men.

His name, as I knew from previous encounters, was Detective Sergeant Matthews, of the Dedley CID and, although he had achieved that status some time after Robin had left both it and Dedley behind him and moved on to higher things at Scotland Yard, they were well acquainted and their paths still crossed from time to time.

For this reason, both Toby and I expected and received rather more deference than was accorded to the average interviewee and, having first apologised for the late call, Matthews then, with barely a second's hesitation, accepted the offer of a drink.

'I am sure you must be in need of it,' Toby said, pouring out a lavish whisky. 'I gather from Mrs Parkes that there was some unpleasantness on the Common this afternoon and I expect you have been on the go ever since?'

'About sums it up, sir, although unpleasant would be by way of an understatement.'

'And this is your last call, I take it?'

'That's right,' the Sergeant agreed, tapping his glass to underline the message. 'I was with Mr and Mrs Parkes earlier on and she told me you'd be at home all evening, so I thought I'd best get the others over first. Just routine in your case, of course, but if you would be so good as to fill me in with one or two facts, to keep the records straight, I'd be grateful.'

'Oh, but naturally. Glad to help in any way we can, aren't we, Tessa? Are you going to write things down? If so, perhaps you'd feel more at home in the chair over there beside the table?'

I noticed that Toby was being ultra-gracious and accommodating which, to members of his intimate circle, might have suggested a certain deviousness at work behind the winning smiles, but luckily the Sergeant's knowledge stopped some way short of this and he said:

'Yes, very well. This will only take a minute or two and then I'll leave you in peace. I understand you were both here throughout the afternoon and evening?'

'Quite right, Sergeant. Either in the house or garden.'

'And I take it neither of you went out on the Common at any time between, let's say, two and six o'clock?'

23

'Oh no, otherwise we should have mentioned it, but in fact I make a point of avoiding the Common as far as possible during summer weekends and advising my guests to do the same. You can't move for sweet-wrappings and empty tins, not to mention abandoned cats and dogs. It is one of the penalties of living in an area of outstanding natural beauty.'

'Quite so. And how about the other two? Did they follow your advice?'

'Other two?'

'Mrs Parkes happened to mention that there'd been two ladies from London having lunch here today.'

'Ah yes, friends of Tessa's. They were here at her invitation.'

'And they remained with you the whole time? Didn't leave the premises to take a stroll on their own, for example?'

'Oh no, I don't think so. I don't remember their doing that, do you, Tessa?'

'Oh no.'

'We took our exercise on the croquet lawn, you see. As you know, it is not only an exhausting pastime, but one which requires intense concentration. I am sorry we can't be more helpful, Sergeant, but I daresay it is only what you expected and also that if either of us had noticed anything suspicious, you would have been the first to hear about it.'

'Quite so. As I say, this is by way of being a formality, something which had to be dealt with, seeing how you're situated here. I may want to ask Mrs Price for the names and addresses of her friends in London, but I hardly envisage the need for it at this stage. So I won't keep you any longer. Don't bother to see me out and thanks again for your patience and courtesy.'

'Only sorry we couldn't provide the vital clue as well,' the courteous and patient man replied, adding in a slight descent from these noble heights, 'Oh, by the way, I quite forgot to ask you, who was this woman who's been killed? No one local, I understand?'

'No . . . that's right, not from these parts.'

24

'Well, far be it for me to embarrass you with questions you'd prefer not to answer.'

'I can't see there'd be any harm in you knowing. It'll be in the papers tomorrow, no doubt. Tell you the truth, we had a bit of bother finding out ourselves. Her handbag had been dumped down in the field some distance from where she was found. It only came to light an hour or two ago.'

'Really? How interesting. But how could you tell it was hers? Surely it could belong to some quite different woman, who is still alive and wondering where she dropped it?'

'Not this one. It was really more of a briefcase than a lady's handbag. Of course, there's no saying what articles may have been removed from it, but there was quite a lot left, including a sleeveless jacket of the same material as the silk dress she was wearing.'

'There now! How very convenient.'

'You could say that. Another bonus was a leather notecase. No money in it, which tells its own tale, perhaps, but it contained numerous identification documents. Credit cards, driving licence, passport, the lot. She was a Mrs Barbara Landauer, journalist by profession.'

'Passport, did you say? Wasn't that rather an odd thing to take on a Sunday outing to the country?'

'Oh, I don't know. Perhaps she thought her bag was the safest place for it, poor lady. She was American, you see. We checked it with her embassy and it appears she was over here on business. Just what she was doing in this part of the world and whether she came on her own, or with someone else, is something we still have to find out.'

25

5

Mrs Parkes's morning routine was unvaried. She left her flat over the garage and set to work on Toby's breakfast at precisely eight thirty. So when my alarm clock woke me at eight, I gathered my wits about me and staggered down to the hall to put through a call to the New Westminster Hotel.

It was as well that I had allowed myself plenty of time because Lorraine needed a good chunk of it for wit-gathering of her own, having instantly concluded, when woken by the bell, that the hotel was on fire.

'Now, steady yourself, Lorraine and try to take this in because it's important and I haven't got all day,' I said, cutting her short. Whereupon she showed her true worth by replying briskly: 'Go ahead, I'm listening.'

'Do you think you could duck out of the Baker Street ramble, get on a train to Oxford and meet me for lunch?'

'Why not? What time, and where will I find you?'

'I'll leave a message at the stage door. They'll let me know when you arrive and I'll get down there as soon as I can.'

'OK. By important, do you mean bad news?'

'Not necessarily, but I think it's something you ought to know about. I'll explain when I see you.'

'You know what I think?' she asked when I had outlined the events of the previous evening over plates of lasagne in a brightly lit dungeon off St Giles called the Casa Oliviera and known to us simple-minded Thespians as Castor Oil.

'Think about what?'

'Mrs Parkes. I think there's something funny going on there. Why would she pick on Robin to convey the message that she had a damn good idea that Bev had been out on the Common yesterday afternoon at just around the time when that woman was killed, and then say nothing about it when the police questioned her? According to you, she didn't even mention that the two guests had come via London from America and yet she must have known that Robin would pass it all on to you. So what's her game? Smells like blackmail to me.'

'Well, to be fair, Lorraine, none of us knew at that stage that Mrs Landauer was also from America, so it wouldn't have mattered what nationality you were. Still, I can understand you feeling as you do because there does seem to be the whiff of a veiled threat hanging around. However, you may be relieved to hear that Toby, who ought to know, doesn't see it in that light at all.'

'Oh no? Which way does he see it?'

'Well, he's inclined to be the tiniest bit cynical, as you know, but I daresay he's got it right this time. His explanation is that it all stems from what he calls the Parkes power complex.'

'I don't care for the sound of that either.'

'Well, I suppose you could call it moral blackmail, in a sense. He maintains that she doesn't want him to forget that she never misses a trick and could fill a book with precise and accurate details of his private life. At the same time, she would no more dream of showing such a book to anyone outside those four walls, including the entire police force and inner Cabinet, even under physical duress, than of taking up domestic employment with an Arab terrorist. The reasoning behind this being as follows: in the first place, it would conflict with her image of herself as the world's one and only female Jeeves. Secondly, it would diminish her own status to be employed by a man who, however blameless, was careless enough to become involved in sordid scandals of a criminal nature. It is therefore his conviction that we can safely rely on Mrs Parkes to see all, hear all, and repeat nothing. I told you he was cynical.'

27

'Well, I'm not. I'm sentimental and over-emotional through and through,' Lorraine announced with a certain pride, becoming heated and tearful at the same time, as though to prove her point, 'and, if you really want to know, I consider his opinions on the subject to be pure fish wallop.'

I did not correct her because Lorraine and I have always kept up a private game of talking each other's language, when together, and I feel sure I commit at least as many gaffes in hers as she does in mine.

'I'd have the ice-cream, if I were you,' I said, handing her the menu. 'It's bound to be good here.'

'And might help to cool me down, you mean?'

'Well, it did just strike me, Lorraine, that it wasn't so much the fact that Mrs Parkes might know a thing or two that we were disputing, but whether she could be trusted to keep it to herself.'

'So?'

'So it now begins to sound as though she might also know something else, which she hasn't even hinted at, but which you already suspect yourself.'

'Heavens no. As though there could be anything. . . . Wasn't I with you and Toby every living minute of the day. How would I know anything that you two don't?'

'But you do seem worried.'

'Worried, worried? No, I'm not. What would I have to be worried about? I don't think I want any ice-cream. Let's just settle for coffee, shall we?' she asked, as the waitress hovered.

'OK. Two coffees, please, and the bill.'

'What would I have to be worried about?' Lorraine repeated when our plates had been removed.

'Beverly, presumably. How was she last night, after I spoke to you? Everything back to normal?'

'Well, for God's sake, Tessa, weren't you the one who warned me against making judgements of that kind? Did you, or did you not, advise me to lay off looking for oddities in her behaviour and simply treat her like any other bright, but fairly unsophisticated, girl who's in Europe without her parents for the very first time?'

'Yes, I did, but I only meant that it might be a mistake to analyse everything she said and did in the light of her past history and keep watching for signs of an imminent relapse.'

'Then all I can say is, you appear to have changed your mind.'

'Up to a point I suppose that's true, but you must admit that this new development has put a rather different complexion on things. I doubt if I'd have dragged you all the way up here to talk about it, if it hadn't been for that curious remark of Beverly's you told me about.'

'What curious remark?'

'Oh, you can't have forgotten. It was when you told her that you didn't believe in ghosts and that when people were dead they were dead, full stop. Did I dream it, or did she not then say that she hadn't been talking about a dead person, but one who was still alive?'

'No, you didn't dream it.'

'So I wondered if there'd been any more remarks of that kind? Whether she'd referred to the subject again?'

'No, she didn't.'

'In that case, nothing to worry about. As I said at the time, it was probably just a bit of fanciful showing off, and which has turned out to be quite an unfortunate coincidence. I apologise for making such a drama of it.'

'You're crazy, I'm the one to apologise. I seem to have made a mess of things ever since I took this job on and quarrelling with you is the last way to put it right. Do you have time for some more coffee?'

'No, thanks, I'll make do with this, but you go ahead if you want to. I can always leave you, if necessary. What sort of a mess do you feel you've made?'

'One reason why Beverly didn't mention the ghost again is that she didn't get the chance. She wasn't back in the hotel until God knows what time and, as far as I know, she went straight to her room. She was still in it, with the *Do Not Disturb* sign hanging on the doorknob when I came out this morning.'

'Oh, I see! So Virginia and Ed decided it was their turn to take over the supervising? About time!'

'No, they didn't. They weren't back till late either, but they didn't have Beverly with them.'

'Well, for God's sake, Lorraine, I call that too bad.'

'It wasn't their fault. Not entirely, anyway. They spent yesterday at Windsor, like the good little American tourists they are and, when they'd had lunch and done the Doll House and the Chapel, they took a trip on one of those river steamers. After a couple of hours of that they were about ready to go back to London, so they disembarked at some small place about ten miles upriver. I forget the name of it, but they'd checked that it had a train station and that it only took just over an hour to Paddington. Only snag was it was closed. No trains on Sundays. That meant finding a cab to take them to some other place where they did have trains running. Funny thing is, it turned out to be Storhampton, so they could have had a ride home with us, if we'd known.'

'Even a train from Storhampton must have got them home before midnight?'

'I guess so, but it wasn't their lucky evening because they found they'd just missed one train and there wasn't another for over an hour. They weren't about to hang around the station all that time, so they went into the town and found a place to eat. After that, they just managed to get on the last train at ten o'clock. You can't exactly blame them, Tessa. They're both pretty young themselves, not much older than Beverly and, after all, I was supposed to be in charge.'

'Yes, I know, and therefore I assume you're not going to tell me that you let Beverly go buzzing off on her own?'

'You're darn right I'm not. Might have been better if I had.'

I looked at my watch. 'Listen, Lorraine, I don't wish to sound ungracious, but still less do I want to lose my hard-earned reputation for punctuality. If there's something you want to tell

30

me, or think I might be able to advise you about, could you spit it out fairly quickly?'

'Yes. No. What time will you be through?'

'Rehearsing? Five, five thirty.'

'OK, I'll meet you back in the hotel around five thirty.'

'Now, listen, you can't hang around Oxford for over three hours.'

'Sure I can, I'll be fine. I want to spend some time at the bookstore and I've been told about a place where they have cashmere sweaters to make your eyes pop. Not forgetting the museum. Henry would never forgive me if I didn't visit the museum.'

'In that case, I have a better idea. I'll come up to London with you and spend the night there. It'll make a nice surprise for Robin and you can lay bare your soul on the train. It's becoming the accepted way of passing the time on the journey between London and Oxford.'

6

A pristine and plush-looking limousine drew up at the kerb as I reached the steps to the hotel entrance, but I gave it no more than a passing glance, being eager to get my hands on the local evening paper, which I knew would be on sale in the foyer.

The murder at Roakes Common took up most of the front page, although the text only occupied half as much space as the headlines. I was skimming through it when my attention was diverted by the sight of the revolving doors spinning round, as though they had been caught up in a whirlwind, which in a sense they had, since Lorraine, never the most patient of women, had propelled them forward with such force as to take her past her stopping place, thus obliging her to make the circuit twice, to the great displeasure of an elderly man who had been attempting to leave the building.

'How was I to know they'd be made of plastic?' she demanded. 'They look solid enough.'

'Oh, they're a modern innovation. Probably weren't installed until about forty years ago.'

'Didn't you hear me yelling at you?'

'No. When was that?'

'Outside, in that car I've rented. I wanted to give you a surprise and all you did was walk right on as though you were stone deaf. Are you all set and ready to go?'

'Not quite. I don't need to pack anything, but I want to tell Reception I won't be back till tomorrow and I also have to ask them to look up a train for us.'

'No, you don't, we're going by car. I've rented it for the

evening and he'll drive you back tomorrow, if you want. It's OK, no need to look so horrified. The car has to be returned to the depot tomorrow anyway, so you may just as well be in it and the driver won't mind one bit. His name is Basil and he has a sister-in-law living in Fulham, where he can spend the night.'

'Really, Lorraine, you overwhelm me. Marriage to Henry certainly seems to have changed you. I never noticed this highly organised, bossy streak before.'

'It's Henry's money that's done it,' she explained. 'Being rich has changed my whole outlook. I have to keep dreaming up all sorts of new and interesting ways to spend it and that takes organisation, if you don't want to fall behind. Want me to fix it with Reception for you?'

'No, thanks. Poor I may be, but I can manage that much on my own.'

'What did you make of that?' I asked, pointing to the newspaper, when we were in the car.

The ebullient phase had passed and she was back in the scowling, withdrawn mood which had been in evidence earlier in the day.

'Doesn't tell us much, does it? Just that there's to be an inquest on Wednesday and a man was held for questioning at Dedley police station for several hours and then turned loose.'

'Yes, Jimmie Peacock, the local bad boy.'

'Killer, you mean?'

'Not up to now and I doubt if he had any hand in this one. He's been in the nick once or twice, but only for petty crime. Stealing car radios, disguising himself as the gasman in order to cosh old ladies and grab their savings from the teapot, that sort of thing. Added to which, he may well have been lurking somewhere near the scene of the crime yesterday. Plenty of pickings to be had on the Common on a fine Sunday, people being careless about locking their cars when they go for a stroll and so on.'

'Don't you find it strange, Tessa, that neither he nor anyone else seems to have noticed anything suspicious?'

'Perhaps Jimmie did and he may have told the police about it, for all we know, in which case they could even now be following it up. On the other hand, perhaps someone else, some innocent picnicker from faraway Rickmansworth or Maidenhead, noticed something but has reasons of his own for not coming forward. If that were so, I don't see how they would ever catch up with the murderer. Tell me something, Lorraine, I know this is a fatuous question, with a population of two hundred thousand million people or whatever it is, but have you, by any chance, ever heard of this Barbara Landauer?'

'OK, being a fatuous question, I'll give you the same answer it usually gets, which is yes.'

'You don't mean you've actually met her?'

'Not me, no, but if she's the same one, and I suppose she has to be, I do know people who have.'

'Is that because she's a well-known journalist, or just coincidence?'

'Neither of those. I didn't know she was a journalist, but if it's true, she was probably over here on some special assignment from one of the magazines. She's done a number of things in her time and she's been around for years.'

'And when you say you know people who've met her, would that include members of the Finkelstein family?'

'I honestly couldn't tell you, but, if so, she'd have dropped them by now.'

'Because they're no longer rich?'

'Right.'

'Did Henry know her?'

'I doubt it. She wasn't his type. Any more questions?'

'Plenty, but I don't imagine you know the answer to the most important one any more than I do, although it's doubtless the one you've spent the last ten minutes asking yourself. However, if we talked about that all the way back to London, we still shouldn't come any nearer to making up our minds whether Beverly's remark about the ghost could have been inspired by

34

the fact that at some point in her life she'd met Barbara Landauer. So let's drop that for the moment and get back to the subject we were discussing at lunch. Where did she spend yesterday evening, if not with her sister and brother-in-law? And, wherever it was, did she go with or without your blessing?'

'Hard to judge in a court of law. The jury could come down on either side.'

'Oh, Lorraine, do stop being so cryptic. What's the law got to do with it?'

'Nothing, I guess. What happened was that there's this couple in our group called Neilsen, which is all wrong for a start, because she's the one who matches up to everyone's idea of a typical Scandinavian. Very tall and blonde and also very severe. She hardly ever smiles, but she's watchful and she talks in kind of growls. Know what I mean?'

'Yes, I do. And he?'

'Exact opposite. Never stops talking and laughing and kind of nudging and he's more Spanish- or Italian-looking than anyone with that name has a right to be. He's tactile, too. Comes up very close when he's talking to you and grabs your arm just to tell you it's stopped raining now. I don't understand what they're doing on this trip because neither seems to know much more than I do about mystery fiction, but someone told me he'd had a heart attack a while back, so perhaps they just picked one out of the hat. Or maybe he's one of those people who couldn't enjoy just any old cruise, where you look at the ocean and play deck quoits. He can't relax for a second. He told me he owns three different companies in three separate states and he spends most of his time flying about between them and turning them all into goldmines.'

'What they call a workaholic?'

'Oh, sure. With jog and golf and a few other holics thrown in. He says his handicap is plus one and he's a philatelist in his spare time.'

'And they're the people who took Beverly out last night?

They sound bizarre, but relatively harmless, and they appear to have got her home safely, so what are you worried about?'

'It wasn't as simple as that. As soon as we were back in the hotel, I told Bev I was planning on a shower and change of clothes and she should come to my room in about an hour, when we'd decide where to eat and how to spend the evening. She was late arriving and she told me she'd run into Mr Neilsen on her way there and they'd made this plan for us to go and see some horror movie from outer space. It was full of hairy monsters who trampled down forests and skyscrapers like they were blades of grass. It was playing out at Hampstead, or somewhere, and I certainly wasn't about to go all that way just to sit through two hours of that. I said if she wanted to she'd better go ahead on her own.'

'And who shall blame you?'

'I don't know who else, but I do blame myself. I should have been paying closer attention, but she talks so fast and it all comes rushing out when she's in that mood. Anyway, I'd gathered the impression that there'd be the three of them in this party, the two Neilsens and Beverly. Well, wouldn't you have?'

'I expect so.'

'So I gave her my blessing, told her to have a nice evening and I'd see her in the morning. To be quite honest, and this is where the remorse really hits, I felt relieved to be free of her company for a few hours.'

'Quite understandable, but when did you learn the bitter truth?'

'Not until around eleven. By then I'd been to a movie myself, one I'd already seen with Henry, which was a mistake because it made me feel more homesick than ever. The desk clerk handed me a note, along with my key. It was a message from Virginia, who'd called to explain why they wouldn't be back till late. I was reading it when I walked into the elevator and I didn't do more than barely glance at the two or three other people who went in ahead of me. Then it stopped at the third or fourth storey and a woman wearing a raincoat got out, and I realised it was Mrs Neilsen. The doors were beginning to close and I called out "How was it?", or something or other, and I'm not even sure whether she heard me. I have a kind of idea that she turned round and there was a funny sort of expression on her face, kind of blank, but I could have put that in myself when I was going through it all in my mind during the night. At the time I just concluded that they'd all come in ahead of me and that Bev was already asleep. It wasn't until I woke up in the night and started going over it that it hit me what really must have been going on right there under my nose and what a fine mess I was making of my guardianship.'

'So what did you do?'

'Called the switchboard and asked them to find out if Miss Finkelstein was in Room 881 yet. They must have thought I was crazy, I guess, because they're probably not used to having questions of that kind fired at them at three o'clock in the morning, but they told me her key wasn't there, which was all I needed. They have these new-fangled keys that set off a screaming noise if you take them outside the hotel, so I knew she must have come in.'

'And so all was well?'

'Far as it went. Then this morning, after I spoke to you, I went by her room and there was this *Do Not Disturb* notice on the door, which hadn't been there the night before. So back I go to my own room, pick up the phone and tell them to keep ringing until she answered and eventually, well, around five or six minutes later, she did answer.'

'How did you handle it?'

'More restrained than I felt, I tell you. I asked her if she'd enjoyed the evening and she said, yes, it had been great. She sounded OK, quite normal and relaxed, just annoyed with me for waking her up to say something like that. I told her it was a good thing I had, because she was supposed to be downstairs with the rest of the party by ten o'clock, waiting for the bus to pick them up and, since I'd planned to spend today with you, she'd be on her own. There didn't seem any use in questions or recriminations. If she'd behaved stupidly, it wouldn't help for her to feel I was spying on her and, if she hadn't, it could have done a lot of harm. So all I did after that was call Virginia and impress on her that she and Ed would be in charge and to stick with her through every minute until I came back. I didn't say a word to her about last night either. She'd only have started prancing around on her high horse and saying "I told you so" and that wouldn't have helped anything either. But I was getting to the pitch where I had to unloose to someone about it, so why not you? That's why, failing the Hope Diamond, I owe you this trip to London.'

'And I'm glad you told me, Lorraine, because, as usual, you're letting it run away with you. It has to be all or nothing, that's the only way you can function, I realise that, but I honestly do think you're making too much of this particular episode. Very likely, it was a perfectly innocent misunderstanding about Mrs Neilsen not being included in the party. But even if there had been an element of deceit, so what? Beverly doesn't seem to have come to any harm and you say she was quite normal when you spoke to her this morning, so I can't see you have very much to worry about and I bet Henry would agree with me.'

'Maybe you're right, but the trouble is that neither of you was there and I still feel uneasy. Like there was something I'd missed, or still can't see the significance of. I don't like Mr Neilsen either, although I still can't figure out why.'

'Well, tell me a bit more about him. What sort of age is he?'

'Oh, about the same as me. Fifty something, I guess.'

'Don't be absurd, you're not fifty anything.'

'I know that, sweetheart, I'm thirty-nine-and-three-quarters, but right now I feel fifty. Or maybe fifteen would be closer,' she added sadly. 'It's no good, Tessa, you'll have to form your own opinion of him and his wife too. I can't wait to hear it, if you want to know.'

'You'll have to wait some time, though, won't you? I thought you told me you wouldn't be in Oxford until the weekend after next?'

'Oh, that! Yes,' she replied in a surprisingly offhand way, considering her former impatience.

'Where do you go next? I've lost track.'

'Bath. We spend two nights there and then go to Cornwall, which is Christie country, so they tell me.'

'That I knew, but I don't connect anyone well-known with Bath.'

'It turns out there's some writer who lives there and uses it for background, as well. Edith tells me he's very popular in the States. His books are all about murder in the Pump Room in the first century and he's going to take us on a tour where a lot of them happened. That way we'll be having fun and getting some history thrown in as a bonus. An offer no good American could resist.'

'Who's Edith?'

'A fellow traveller. You'll mee ... Oh, there I go! I'm beginning to feel like a criminal myself. Someone could organise a tour round me and charge money for it.'

'You're not still on about last night? I thought we'd settled all that?'

'No, this is something else. Something you said a while back.'

'What, in particular?'

'How I'd need to wait for your verdict on the Neilsens. I'm hoping it won't be necessary, only I forgot to explain why and you may not like it. After I'd fixed up for Basil to drive us into London, I got another great idea and called Beacon Square. Robin wasn't there, I hadn't expected him to be, but I spoke with your Mrs Cheeseman and she said she'd leave a message for him, so he'd see it as soon as he came in.'

'Risky thing to do, as you'd know if you'd ever had to make head or tail of one of her messages. What was this one about?'

'Inviting him round to the hotel for a drink this evening. I figured he'd be resigning himself to just another lonely evening, with no one to warm his slippers, and he might jump at it.'

'Oh, I see. At least, I begin to.'

'OK, I suppose it was a juvenile trick, but I thought it would be fun to see his face when he walked in and, instead of just me, you'd be there as well. What do you say?'

'That it was the worst idea you ever had. If he were to walk in and see me looking as scruffy as I do at this minute, he'd probably walk right out again. Do you realise that I've been rehearsing solidly for about eight hours and hadn't even had time to comb my hair when you came roaring up in your golden chariot? If you think I'd allow Robin, or anyone else including your friend Mr Neilsen, anywhere near me until I've tarted myself up, you could easily be mistaken.'

'Well, yes,' she admitted, after an appraising look. 'That's not such a bad idea. After the build-up I've given you, we don't want them to feel let down. I'll drop you off at your place and send Basil back for you in an hour. How's that?'

'Have to do, I suppose.'

'And you will come, won't you? Promise me!'

'Oh yes, you may depend on it, Lorraine. I make a point of never standing in the path of a bulldozer.'

7

'And crafty with it,' Robin remarked, as we proceeded in hushed grandeur along the eight hundred yards to our destination. 'My instructions were to ring the hotel as soon as I came in and leave a message for her. Naturally, I wasn't prepared for you to come marching in only half an hour later. If I'd known that would happen, she'd have had a very different message from me. A cosy domestic evening is just what my arid life needs.'

'Cheer up, Robin. We shan't have to stay long, just make ourselves agreeable for half an hour or so. There'll still be plenty of the night left for the cosy domestic bit.'

'It still seems an awful waste of time and, speaking of waste, how about the lunacy of sending this vulgar great hearse to collect us? We could have walked it in five minutes. It will take twice as long to drive through all this traffic.'

'I expect she was afraid we should make some excuse to back out. Sending Basil was one more way of tightening the knot.'

'Which is exactly what I meant by crafty.'

'Oh, don't be too hard on her,' I said. 'Admittedly, she does seem to be catching the disease which afflicts so many of the rich, causing them to believe that everyone else will fall in with their wishes as a matter of course, but you can't deny that her motives are unselfish. She's trying to protect someone else and that always brings out the whirlwind streak. She'll stop at nothing to get us all to lay down our lives for her friend.'

'The friend this time being Beverly?'

'Yes, of course.'

'But why is it necessary to go to such lengths on her behalf? There's nothing you or I could do to stop the silly girl making an ass of herself with some man twice her age, even if we felt disposed to try, which personally I don't. And, anyway, there's no particular reason why the flirtation, or whatever it is, should end in catastrophe.'

'I think that's only part of the story. I'm not convinced that she believes herself that Beverly needs protection from him as much as she does from herself.'

'So what you really mean, I suppose,' Robin said, as Basil glided to a stop at the exact stop where the commissionaire's outstretched hand was level with the doorhandle, 'is that, although nothing would make her admit it, she is privately of the opinion that Beverly did see someone she knew on the Common yesterday afternoon, and she is spinning round in circles in case Henry finds out and blames her for what may come of it.'

'In a nutshell,' I replied, gathering my skirts and stepping forth towards the maelstrom, 'that's the nub, I shouldn't wonder.'

In fact, once past the imposing glass doors, it was rather like walking into an enormous, brand-new theatre-in-the-round. The whole expanse of ground floor was laid out before us and in the centre of it there was a circular raised platform, more brilliantly lit than the surrounding area. On a smaller dais within it, stage right, a young man in white tie and tails was tinkling out popular tunes of the thirties on a grand piano, much of which was concealed behind a wealth of waxy-looking foliage and flowers, banked up in tiers of gondola-shaped, gold-painted baskets. Several dozen members of the cast were already assembled here, although neither Lorraine nor Beverly was among them.

The rest of the floor space consisted of a wide circular promenade, whose outer perimeter was lined with an unbroken display of boutiques, chemists, souvenir shops, florists, tourist information desks and bureaux de change. It was designed to cater for every whim except that, so far as we could ascertain from one complete circuit, there was absolutely no one of whom we could enquire as to the whereabouts of our hostess, or who might conceivably convey the message that her guests had arrived.

The reception desk, which had seemed to be the obvious answer and which we eventually tracked down in a side lane behind the gaudy merchandise, proved to be a total loss. It was manned by some half-dozen elegant young women, who were tapping out messages on computers, in the intervals between disappearing into the back office with sheaves of papers in their hands and grave expressions on their faces, as though important news had just come in from Nicaragua. None of them had more than an occasional hurried word to spare for the group of people who were waiting to make, or, as would have seemed more logical, cancel their reservations.

'Come on, then!' Robin said, a gleam of hope lighting up the tragic mask. 'We can always say we spent half an hour trying to find her and then concluded we'd come to the wrong hotel.'

'You know we can't,' I reminded him. 'Basil is in her pay, if not her thrall, and would have no scruples about letting us down.'

'Yes, I suppose you're right. What a way to run a brothel,' he added gloomily, quoting a saying he had picked up from his father at an early age and had had frequent recourse to in times of stress ever since.

'Where the hell have you two been?' Lorraine demanded, bearing down on us at this point, with sparks flying from her eyes. 'I've been chasing all over for you. Basil called in to report twenty minutes ago and I was beginning to think you'd walked out on me.'

'Oh no, what a ridiculous idea,' I replied before Robin could speak. 'It was my silly fault for not finding out your room number in advance. Never mind, we did a nice bit of window-shopping while we waited.'

'So, if you're through now, let's go, shall we?'

'Where to?'

'My room. They're all waiting for you.'

'Who's all?' I enquired, as we dawdled away another five or six minutes staring at a row of lighted red and green arrows, whose promise was not fulfilled.

'Well, let's see now. Virginia and Ed and Beverly, of course, and the Neilsens, that weird couple I was telling you about. And then there's Edith Dearing and her niece, Marilou. You're going to love Mrs Dearing. She's crippled, which is why she has to have Marilou along wherever she goes, but she's a wild fan of yours. She comes from Missouri,' Lorraine added as though to clinch the matter, then, changing tack, she said: 'Gosh, it's good to see you again, Robin. I was beginning to forget what it was like to have a real man around.'

It provided a perfect example of how flattery can bring out the best in people because a moment later one set of lift doors began slowly sliding apart and, judging correctly that they would instantly close again at twice the speed, Robin flung himself forward to intercept this process and stood waiting for us to precede him inside in the manner of one nonchalantly holding up the Tower of Pisa.

'It must be quite a large room then,' I suggested as we marched down a corridor on the sixth floor and I glanced apprehensively at the doors to the left and right of us, which seemed to be set perilously cheek by jowl.

'It's one great enormous suite, honey, just you wait and see. "Well, that's quite unnecessary," I told Henry. "We'll only be there three nights and why would I want to rattle around in a suite all on my own? I can only sleep in one room at a time." But he insisted and he was right, as usual. We use it all the time. You can't imagine the kind of people you're liable to run into in that circus ring downstairs.'

'Aren't they mostly American?' Robin asked, descending a notch or two from his former heights of chivalry.

'Sure they are, that's what makes us cringe. We hardly ever

meet people like that back home. It's terrible to discover the reason is that they're all away on trips to Europe.'

'We all feel like that when we meet our fellow countrymen abroad,' I assured her.

'Yes, I guess I've led a sheltered life up till now. Always staying with you and Robin when I come over.'

'So, one way and another,' Robin remarked, as she removed a large plastic card from her bag and inserted it into the slit above the doorhandle of Number 679, 'this trip is providing you with a complete new range of experience.'

'Yes, it is,' she agreed, with a return of the sombre mood. 'And am I thankful to have you two here to take some of the load off me this evening. Don't imagine I'm not grateful.'

Describing it as a suite was no exaggeration. Indeed, a suite and a half would have been nearer the mark, since, in addition to the sitting room on the right of the hall, which itself was large enough to accommodate ten or twelve people, there was an alcove on one side of it, presumably behind the bathroom, which served as a respectable-sized dining room.

Both Neilsens were instantly recognisable from Lorraine's description, Mrs particularly because she had emphasised her snow maiden personality by seating herself in an upright chair, as remote as space would allow from the rest of the company. Her husband, on the other hand, was in the thick of it and we had heard his laughter and raised voice from outside the room. He and Beverly were seated close together on a sofa, with their backs to us, as we went in and I could sense a stiffening in Lorraine as she took in the scene, which showed Mr Neilsen's right arm draped across the cushion behind Beverly so that, had she leaned backwards, she would have found herself in a highly compromising position.

Ed and Virginia were also easy to pick out. She was tall, slim and patrician-looking, with thick, shining and well-brushed auburn hair, a darker and more becoming shade than her sister's, while Ed was over six feet, with honest blue eyes and a

45

mouthful of dazzling teeth. Had he been wearing white shorts and brandishing a tennis racquet, he would have been snapped up on the spot by any advertising agency worth its salt as an all-purpose model for everything from life insurance to deodorants. And, had I been taking part in a 'Pick the Right Name' competition, I should have had no hesitation in choosing Ed and Virginia.

Mrs Dearing was easily identifiable too, as the angular old party, with the face of a benevolent horse and a walking stick propped against the side of her chair. Her hands had become twisted and misshapen by arthritis, but evidently this caused her no embarrassment for she was wearing an outsize cabochon diamond in a very ornate setting on one of them, which effectively drew attention to it. Despite her handicap, she had a friendly, alert and amused expression, which made her as attractive in her way as the stately Virginia.

This only left one member of the party to be accounted for, so, inevitably, the seriously overweight and pasty-faced young woman sitting between Virginia and Mrs Neilsen, but speaking to neither, was the niece, Marilou.

With the exception of these three, they all bounded to their feet as we entered and, having followed his own introduction by a particularly loud and clear repetition of his name, Mr Neilsen not only explained to me at length why this encounter was likely to rank as the high point of his trip, but kept a tight grip of my hand while he was doing it. He added that he was breathtaken to discover the impossible truth that the vision in reality could turn out to be superior to the screen image, thus removing the last vestige of doubt that, for the time being anyway, high-flying actresses were rather more his cup of tea than high-ranking policemen.

I find it hard to dislike people who talk that kind of nonsense, however brash and insincere, and would have been willing to put up with several more minutes of it. However, I was aware that it was not within my terms of reference to get stuck into a conversation of this kind so early in the proceedings. My role

46

was to be that of spectator, observing him from a distance and, in particular, assessing his intentions, if any, towards Beverly. So as soon as he had bustled off to the dining alcove to fetch me a glass of the Dom Perignon with which Lorraine, no doubt acting on instructions from Henry, kept herself well stocked, I strolled across and seated myself in the vacant chair beside Mrs Dearing and asked her how she was enjoying the trip.

'It's just wonderful,' she replied. 'And now we have the pleasure of meeting you, Miss ... Oh, now wait a minute, I have to get this right. Are you Miss Crichton, or Mrs Robin Price?'

'It depends on the circumstances,' I explained. 'In this case, I should think Tessa would be the most appropriate, if that's all right with you?'

'That'll do fine. I gather you and Lorraine are old friends?'

'Yes, we are.'

'She's a wonderful person.'

'I agree.'

'And, from all I hear,' Mrs Dearing remarked drily, 'Henry is another.'

She reminded me so sharply of the forthright, elderly women who masterminded the coffee mornings and tombolas in aid of the church and village hall at Roakes Common, that I felt emboldened to speak as freely as though we had known each other for years.

'I hope you won't mind my asking,' I said, glancing down at her footstool, 'but I find it amazing that you would choose a holiday of this kind. Isn't it awfully hard to keep up with the rest of the group on these marathon expeditions?'

'Not all all, my dear, quite the contrary. I have my faithful old wheelchair always close at hand and my faithful niece to guide it. It is one of those folding contraptions and it goes wherever I go. Marilou and I are often right out ahead of the rest of them. She's lost a few pounds already, so I don't have to feel too guilty about her doing all the hard work.'

'Oh, I see. It sounds a splendid arrangement. I'll be tempted

47

to try the same dodge myself next time I land at Heathrow and visualise all those miles of walking that lie between me and freedom.'

I was sorry to see that for a moment Mrs Dearing's expression resembled that of a horse which had been given tealeaves instead of bran for supper and it struck me, rather late in the day, that she was probably in a good deal of pain and had found my remarks in poor taste. However, before I could think of a graceful way out, she said equably:

'Oh, comfort's not the only advantage. You get to hear some very interesting things when you're tied to a wheelchair.'

'Honestly? I'd have thought it would make any form of eavesdropping rather difficult and complicated.'

'Excuse me saying so, but I fear you have a devious mind, Tessa. I said hear, not overhear.'

'I beg your pardon. What sort of things do you hear?'

'Due to our privileged position, Marilou and I must be the only two who pick up every word that clever young tour operator, Colin, is telling us as we go along. He's such a smart fellow and a mine of information on all kinds of subjects. I could listen to him all night and I do feel I'm getting more for my money than the rest of them, straggling along somewhere behind and stopping every two minutes to take photographs of each other. Colin always speaks nice and slow too, so that I won't miss anything. In that way he's like a lot of otherwise sane and intelligent people.'

'In what way?'

'They're apt to assume that if someone has a physical handicap, she's liable to be hard of hearing too, if not mentally retarded. Did you never notice that?'

'Not consciously perhaps, but now you mention it I'm ashamed to admit that I have caught myself speaking rather loudly to blind people.'

'That's what I mean. And they tell you things too, the kind of things they might think twice about saying to normal folk. They seem to believe you wouldn't really be taking too much of it in and, if you were, no harm could come from it. So you get to hear quite a lot of interesting points of view.'

'And what do you do with them when you've heard them, I wonder? Are you a writer, by any chance?'

Once again I had the fleeting impression that she was displeased, as though finding the last question more impertinent than any that had gone before, and she turned her head away without answering. However, this may have been because her attention had been diverted by Mr Neilsen, who was now bearing down on us with a glass of champagne in each hand.

'Pardon me for the delay,' he said, handing one of them to me, 'but Lorraine had something on her mind which had to be settled that very minute. You know how it is with her?'

'So well,' I replied, although, curiously enough, it had not escaped me that Lorraine had spent the past five minutes deep in conversation with Robin who, since this was their first meeting in several years, was presumably woefully out of date with news of Henry. 'And no need to apologise,' I added, 'I have been most agreeably occupied while I waited.'

'Oh yes, so I see, talking to my favourite girl,' he replied, leaning towards Mrs Dearing and speaking rather loudly.

'Now, don't tell me you're drinking tonight, Corny?' she asked him, 'after all this fine talk of being on the wagon?'

'I know, I know, and that's exactly where I'm staying, but I thought you might let the festive spirit take over for once, since we have something to celebrate. Why don't I put it down on that table beside you, in case you get tempted?'

'You'll do nothing of the kind. I'm surprised at you, Corny. In the first place, if I would so much as touch it with these wretched hands of mine, it would spill all over the table. And in the second place, as I've told you so often, alcohol disagrees with the drugs I have to take to keep going so I'd be obliged if you'd take it out of my sight this very minute.'

'How about taking it to your wife?' I suggested. 'She has an empty glass.'

'Yes, do that,' Mrs Dearing said, 'and you could tell Marilou to make herself useful by handing round some of those canapés Lorraine has all ready for us. Talking makes me feel hungry. No, no, Tessa, not you, you're not here to be made use of. Nor to be monopolised by me either, now I think of it. You run along with Corny and say hello to Mrs Neilsen. She's a most interesting woman and she needs cheering up, by the look of it.'

'Is Corny really your name?' I asked Mr Neilsen when she had got us all hopping about.

'No, that's just Edith's idea of a joke, I guess. My name's Cornelius and that's always been good enough for most people, but she says it doesn't sound right with Neilsen so it has to be Corny and who cares, for God's sake, so long as it makes her happy? She can't get too many laughs in her life. Hi, there, Helen! How you doing?'

'Well, I thank you,' his wife replied in what Lorraine had described as her growly voice. 'Do sit down, please,' she added, pointing to the now vacant chair beside her.

I was extricating myself from her husband's grasp in order to do so when pre-empted by Beverly, who came bounding up waving a tumbler of tomato juice about and spilling some of it on the carpet. Leaning over the back of the chair, she fixed me with an unblinking stare, as though endeavouring to convey some message quite distinct from her words, which were: 'Hi, there, Tessa! There's something I've been dying to ask you.'

'OK, why not now?'

'Well. . . .' she replied, looking expectantly at the Neilsens, as though waiting for them either to go away or cover their ears. When neither of these things happened, I said:

'On the other hand, if it's private and confidential, like whether that actor who is the love of your life is as gorgeous off screen as on, let us step into the dining room for a moment. We can rearrange the smoked salmon into elegant patterns while we talk. Would you mind?' I asked, turning to Mrs Neilsen. 'I'll be back shortly, so please don't go away.'

She gave no sign of intending to, although it seemed for an

instant that her husband was bent on accompanying us. However, she put a restraining hand on his arm, saying in the manner of one bringing an over-exuberant puppy to heel:

'No, stay here, please, Cornelius. You should know by now when you are not wanted.'

'I just can't stand that woman,' Beverly said moodily, having made a start on the rearrangement programme by constructing a three-tiered smoked salmon sandwich and gobbling it up. 'She really depresses me. Doesn't she depress you?'

'Not particularly, but so far I haven't exchanged more than two sentences with her.'

'No one else has either, and that's how she wants to keep it. She would hate to have someone getting to know her and discovering things about her, and the weird thing is I've seen her somewhere before. She says that's not true, but I know I have.'

These words had the effect of a great light illuminating all the hidden corners and I could not wait to pass on the good news to Lorraine.

'Part of your worry at least is over,' I should tell her. 'It is probably a side effect from all the drugs and only a passing phase, but just at present Beverly is suffering from the delusion that everyone she sees for the first time is someone she has seen before. So there we have the explanation for her remark about the live ghost. No need to see anything sinister in it or to conclude that she went beyond the garden fence. I daresay all she saw was Mr Parkes at work on one of the hedges and in her present rather confused state of mind, she mistook him for her father's attorney.'

At this point in our imaginary conversation Lorraine raised the objection which had by now occurred to me, so I explained it away for both of us by saying:

'No, of course, in theory he doesn't clip hedges on Sunday. Not even Toby would expect that, but Mr Parkes likes to keep

51

an eye on us while we're out there on the loose in his precious garden and a little well-planned job like that gives him a good vantage point.'

Having resolved the matter, I turned my attention back to Beverly and saw that she was looking at me with a somewhat speculative expression.

'Sorry, Beverly, did you say something?'

'I certainly did, but I'm not surprised you didn't hear me. You looked like you'd gone into another world. Maybe you should tell your analyst about it before it gets a hold on you.'

'I'll consider it, but in the meantime what was it you said that I didn't hear?'

'I asked if you'd found my camera, by any chance?'

'Camera?' I repeated, jumping right out of my other world now. 'What camera?'

'Oh, do hush, Tessa. I don't want anyone to hear. That's why this has to be private. It will ruin everything if they hear us.'

'OK, let's start from the beginning in low murmurs. You have lost your camera?'

'Yes, my very own, darling camera. My Daddy gave it to me just before Virginia's wedding. It had a beautiful gold chain attached to it, so I could wear it around my neck. It was the very last present I ever had from him and it made Virginia mad. She thought she was the only one who should be getting expensive gifts. I think I must have left it at your cousin's house yesterday.'

'How do you know you must?'

'Because I was wearing it. I know that for sure because Toby remarked on it. He said he'd never seen one with a gold chain before and it would take a girl like me to possess such a thing. I took that as a real compliment.'

'Which I feel sure was how it was intended. I remember it too, now you mention it, and I'm pretty sure you had it on when you went off on your own after lunch. When did you first miss it?'

'Back at the hotel. I was taking everything out of the bag I carry around with me and it wasn't there.'

'Maybe you left it in the car?'

'No, I didn't. I'm perfectly certain I didn't.'

'Well, you didn't have it round your neck when you were playing croquet, that I do remember, but if you did leave it in Toby's house, there's one thing you can be sure of. Mrs Parkes will find it and she'll know exactly whose property it is.'

'It wouldn't have to be in the house,' Beverly said, going to work on her second sandwich. 'It could have been in the garden.'

'Or on the Common, perhaps?'

'Common?'

'That big open space in front of the house.'

'Oh, there! No, I didn't go walking there, but it could be in the garden.'

'In that case, it may or may not turn up. I'll ask Mr Parkes to keep a lookout for it, by all means, but do explain something, will you, Beverly? Why all the secrecy? Why did we have to come in here and talk about it in hushed whispers?'

'Because I don't want Virginia to know.'

'Whyever not?'

'Because she'd go on and on about it. She noticed right away that I didn't have it with me this morning and I didn't dare tell her I'd lost it. I just said something had gone haywire with the light meter and I'd left it at the hotel camera shop to be fixed. I would buy an ordinary cheap one soon as we arrived at Bath. She's so jealous of that camera because it proved that Daddy loved me best.'

If her deduction was correct, I could not wholeheartedly approve of his taste, but let it pass and said:

'In that case, why should she care if you lost it? If anything, you'd expect her to be pleased.'

'You wouldn't say that if you knew Virginia. It would just about drive her insane to think of something valuable like that going out of the family. She'd be on at me all day long about notifying the insurance company and filling in claim forms and stuff like that.'

'And not such a bad idea, is it? Then you could buy a new one

53

and a new gold chain to go with it, which would be almost as good as getting yours back.'

'No, it wouldn't. It wouldn't be any good at all. It might look the same as the one Daddy chose and bought specially for me, but it wouldn't be the same and it would be so . . . well, sordid, I guess.'

'What's sordid about it, for heaven's sake?'

'Oh, all the grilling I'd get. I remember once when our New York apartment was burglarised, and the way they went on at us you'd have thought we'd done it ourselves. First thing the insurance people wanted to know was whether the police had been notified. Well, look at it my way, Tessa. Who'd want to be dragged into hassles of that kind in a foreign country? Can't you understand what I'm getting at?'

'Oh yes, indeed, Beverly, I do believe I understand perfectly.'

(2)

'And what exactly have you understood?' Robin asked, when Basil had delivered us back at Beacon Square and we were exchanging news and views over plates of bacon and eggs in the kitchen.

'The same as anyone else would, I suppose. Obviously, she's afraid, if not certain, that she did lose the camera on the Common, but the fact that she denies having been there indicates that she saw something or someone which frightened her. I daresay she has now also read something about the murder in a newspaper and has really got the wind up. Or maybe Lorraine mentioned it to her, although I rather doubt it. She's so desperately anxious not to start any more trouble that she's probably keeping her fingers crossed that Beverly will never find out about Mrs Landauer, at least until they're all safely back in the States.'

'Incidentally, Tessa, doesn't it strike you as odd that not one of the others appears to have shown the slightest interest in the murder? Seeing that the victim was American and that two of their party had spent the whole afternoon in the place where it happened, wouldn't you have expected a modicum of curiosity?'

'Not necessarily. I daresay Lorraine never referred to Roakes by name. It wouldn't convey anything to them and she's more likely to have said "a village in Oxfordshire", or just "into the country".'

'Even so, the murder of an American citizen on foreign territory normally creates a certain commotion among the nationals.'

'Oh yes, I grant you, if it had been a hijacking or terrorist attack, but I don't imagine anyone is considering cutting off diplomatic relations on account of this incident. It only rated as a very minor story on an inside page in the London papers and you know yourself how it is, Robin. Very few people bother much with newspapers when they're abroad. They usually just glance at the headlines, to make sure the war hasn't started, and then turn to see what's on at the theatre. It would be different for Beverly, of course. She could well have been on the lookout for something in particular.'

'And, assuming it was something relevant to the murder, don't you feel a twinge of conscience in protecting her?'

'No, none at all.'

'Well, I know all about your loyalty to your friends and how you would feel terrible about letting Lorraine down, but does it still not occur to you that, if Beverly does possess some vital evidence, it might be up to you to find out what it is?'

'The idea did occur to me, but I dismissed it as impractical.'

'Oh, I see.'

'I doubt if you do, Robin, but the fact is that no power on earth would persuade her to confide in me or anyone else, if she has made up her mind not to. I'm sure you're going to tell me that the same could be said of a good many witnesses who are hauled in for questioning and that they can usually be scared or coerced into falling into line, but it wouldn't work here. In the first place, if she persists in denying that she went on the Common yesterday afternoon, there is no way to prove that she is lying. As she had never set foot in the neighbourhood before, there would be no question of anyone having recognised her, so she is quite safe there.'

'Not quite so safe, perhaps, if the camera were to turn up?'

'But it would be a very faint chance, wouldn't it? I suppose someone might have lighted on it among all that scrub and long grass, not to mention dandelions, but it would still be a thousand to one against the finder being honest and public-spirited enough to bother to hand it in at a police station. And, supposing he did, how would they ever connect it with Beverly, unless she had reported its loss? She may have had a mental breakdown, but she's quite sane enough to be able to work that one out.'

'Nevertheless, she did tell you about it.'

'She told me she might have left it in the house or garden. It's just possible that she did, in which case she would dearly like to get it back, if only to head Virginia off. And she must feel that time is on her side there. With any luck, the case will be all wrapped up in a few days, without her being mentioned or involved in any way. Then she'll be able to confess everything to Virginia and explain that she'd been too scared to tell her the truth before.'

'In that case, I should say she's a trifle over-optimistic.'

'Why?'

'Because the mere fact that she is being so cagey about her presence on the Common, plus the enigmatic remark about ghosts who were still alive, indicates that what in fact she saw was someone she knew, or had seen before, who had no business to be there. And that in turn suggests that the murder was not committed by anyone on the wanted list, or a local bad boy like Jimmie Peacock. The chances are that it was a lot more complicated than that and, if so, it's likely to take a hell of a lot longer than two or three days to sort it out.'

'Yes, you're right, of course. I hadn't thought of that. Oh well, they'll just have to fend for themselves as best they can. If the beastly camera should turn up on Toby's premises, he and

Mrs Parkes will know exactly who it belongs to. She makes it her mission in life to let no detail go unnoticed and it appears that Toby remarked on it during lunch. I can't do any more for her and she must manage without me.'

'How many times have I heard those words before, I wonder?' Robin asked, as though talking to himself.

'More than you've had hot dinners, I daresay, but this time is different. For one thing, I shan't be available. They're all off to Bath and points west tomorrow morning. Besides which, with a dress rehearsal and first night looming next week, I shall have other things on my mind. All the same . . .'

'Ah! Here it comes. Par for the course.'

'Nothing sinister. It's only that, in some ways, I shall quite look forward to catching up with them again in Oxford. Apart from Beverly and her missing camera, I'd enjoy another chat with Mrs Dearing. She's a spry old party and it wouldn't surprise me if she had some interesting tales to unfold. And then there's those mysterious Neilsens, of course.'

'What's mysterious about them? As married couples go, I would say they were fairly well balanced. He's manic and she's depressive.'

'I'm not denying that. It's just that . . . oh well, nothing important.'

I had been about to add, but thought better of it in view of his earlier accusation, that, balanced or not, the big question was whether they were a married couple.

8

The curtain went up on the dress rehearsal at six o'clock and, since the scheduled running time was two hours and forty minutes, including a twenty-minute interval, we had hopes of its coming down again at around 11.00 p.m.

They were short-lived, however, and it was after two in the morning when, still in make-up, I lurched out of the hotel lift, then spent about three minutes trying to insert my key into the lock and wondering, were I eventually to succeed, whether I should have the strength to turn it. I was not put to the test, though, because before this point was reached the door was flung open and Robin grabbed my arm and pulled me inside.

'Don't tell me you were in front?' I asked when he had closed it again.

'For a time. They let me sit at the back of the stalls, but I gave up about two hours ago.'

'Why? Weren't you enjoying it?'

'No, I thought it was ghastly and when that wretched Maggie whatever-her-name-is collapsed into floods of tears I couldn't take any more. So I came here, explained my situation, and was given a duplicate key. Anyone could have got away with it, actually. You were lucky not to be confronted by a homicidal maniac when you came in.'

'It's your blunt, honest features which do it,' I told him, 'and no one was ever more glad to see them. Lucky they put me in a double room,' I added, seating myself at the dressing table and going to work with the cold cream. 'I presume you're staying the night?'

'Yes, I'm on my way to Bristol and decided to make a small detour and break the journey here. To tell you the truth, I'd forgotten you had a dress rehearsal this evening. It has rather upset my plans.'

'Never mind. At least, I don't have an early start in the morning. What time do you have to be in Bristol?'

'Not until eleven.'

'Good. Eight hours still left and bags I the bathroom first.'

'How's the Barbara Landauer case coming along?' I asked at breakfast, which, by a rare concession, was brought to our room. 'Did you get a chance to prise anything out of Matthews?'

'Not a lot.'

'But you have spoken to him?'

'Oh yes, I made a point of stopping off at Dedley on my way here, and we had a drink together. He wasn't surprised to see me. Guessing that I'd have heard all about his interview with you and Toby, I think he'd been expecting me hourly.'

'And what did he tell you?'

'Not a lot, as I said. The inquest is down for tomorrow and will be adjourned, pending the usual. The coffin will be flown to America the day after.'

'Surely that can't be all? What was her background and what was she doing over here?'

'The answer to the first question, in a few simple words, is that she'd been through two marriages, both ending in divorce. She was British by birth, but had been living in the States for the past twenty-odd years. She originally went there with her first husband, who was some emigré aristo from a minor European principality. When she ditched him for number two, who was a bona fide American, she became a US citizen and stayed on after that marriage folded too.'

'And the answer to the second?'

'She appears to have no relatives over here, or at any rate to have lost touch with those she had. She arrived unaccompanied

59

on a three-week visit and checked in at a London hotel, where she had reservations for the whole of her stay. She told them she would be travelling around most of the time, but wished to keep her room there as a permanent base.'

'Not the New Westminster Hotel, by any chance?'

'No, I'd have told you straightaway if it had been. That at least might have gone some way to solving the puzzle of Beverly's live ghost.'

'Only a short way, though. I suppose anyone might be midly surprised at seeing a fellow guest from the hotel in such an out-of-the-way place as Roakes, but it would hardly be classed as sensational.'

'From what I hear of Beverly, I wouldn't be too sure of that.'

'OK, but it still wouldn't explain her reluctance to admit she was on the Common herself. However, let's leave her for the moment and get back to Mrs Landauer. What was the purpose of this visit? Not pleasure, I trust?'

'No, she was doing an article for a magazine which carries features about off-the-beaten-track holidays for the rich and jaded. The itineraries include such treats as spending a night in the dungeons of some remote Scottish castle and taking part in the servants' ball in a ducal mansion, with Her Grace and the butler leading the dancing. God knows where they get the servants for these occasions, but I suppose out-of-work actors would go anywhere for a fiver and a free dinner.'

'How fascinating!'

'Oh, do you think so? It all sounds hideously tedious and embarrassing to me.'

'Yes, but it occurs to me that these feature articles could be a not so thinly disguised plug for various pricey tour operators who also specialise in holidays of this kind.'

'Most likely are.'

'Well, that's a link, isn't it? Still, perhaps, too tenuous to engage our attention for the moment. What we really need is a link with Roakes Common. Has there been any progress there?'

'Not much. She appears to have been on her way to a place called Warne Hill which is about twelve miles to the north-west, but no explanation has turned up to account for her having stopped off at Roakes.'

'What happens at Warne Hill?'

'It's a Jacobean manor. The house itself has been knocked about a bit and is of no particular interest, but there's a shoot of nearly six hundred acres. At certain periods during the season, parties of hand-picked guests pay through the nose to rent one of the lodges for the weekend and, under strict supervision of the keepers, to knock off a few pheasants. Everything laid on, I need hardly say, including Edwardian-style picnics for the ladies. Barbara had an appointment to take tea with the owner at four o'clock which, sadly, she was unable to keep.'

'Who is the owner?'

'He's called Sir Mervyn Houghton.'

'Pronounced Hawton.'

'Really? So you do know all about it?'

'It came to me. I didn't make the connection at first because the house is always referred to locally as Warnes, or Mervyn Houghton's place.'

'Have you met him?'

'Yes, several times. Toby knows him well and hates the sight of him.'

'That applies to a good many people Toby knows.'

'I agree, but in this case he has some excuse. Mervyn really is rather a pill. Inbred and raving mad, in all the most unattractive ways. Typical of him to invite someone who's come all the way from America for a cup of tea. He's the meanest man on earth.'

'Well, I daresay that, like a lot of other raving mad and inbred landowners, he's pretty hard up?'

'Not at all, absolutely loaded. His mother was a Miss Pardoe of Pardoes Pickles and Preserves and the house is only run-down because he's too mean to spend money on it. The shoot is kept in immaculate trim because for most of the season it's rented out to syndicates from London and the Persian Gulf.

61

I suppose they don't come so much at weekends, though, and that's why he's put it on the market for American tourists.'

'And is that all he does?'

'Not quite. Curiously enough, he's one of the greatest living authorities on some species of butterfly and he goes to seminars and things like that all over the world, expenses paid, I have no doubt. Would you like to meet him?'

'No, thanks. It's not a subject which I feel could ever get a grip on me and he doesn't sound a particularly attractive character. Besides, the Landauer case is no concern of mine.'

'All the same, I think I might ask Toby to invite him over to lunch on Sunday. He won't be pleased, but I can probably invent some terrible reprisal to threaten him with if he doesn't co-operate.'

'And, apart from his reluctance, what makes you so sure that Houghton won't turn it down?'

'Turn it down? You must be raving. He's like one of those out-of-work actors you were talking about just now. He'd walk barefooted across the Himalayas for a free meal.'

'All right, so one last question. What are you expecting to get out of it?'

'Oh, nothing much, I suppose. He's such a great big, blown-up, pompous snob, though, that I thought it might be fun to try and pin a murder on him.'

'Yes,' Robin admitted with a sigh, 'I was afraid you'd say that.'

Soon after Robin had left for Bristol and while still debating whether to get up and start on some bending and swinging exercises, or stay where I was for another half an hour and read the newspaper, there was a call from Lorraine.

She was in a proper taking, having composed a long and elegantly worded telegram of good wishes for my first night, only to discover that it would not be delivered until the following morning.

'Did you ever hear of anything so dumb in your whole life?' she demanded. 'For God's sake, if I had something to say that could wait till tomorrow, why wouldn't I just put a stamp on and mail it to you? They can't think I'm that rich. So then I had another idea.'

'I'll bet. What was it this time?'

'I was going to find one of those joke telegram firms, you know the kind of thing I mean? I had it all worked out too, how they would do it. Want to hear?'

'Naturally.'

'They would send a man in a white coat, carrying a stretcher, round to the theatre and he would bribe or trick his way into your dressing room. Then he'd tell you he'd been informed by paranormal powers that you'd break a leg this evening and he'd been delegated to be on hand when you did it. How would you have reacted?'

'Hard to say. I suppose I might have asked him how he proposed to carry me out on a stretcher, if there was only one of him, but I doubt if I'd have had the presence of mind. Anyway, that plan didn't work out either?'

'I was afraid, after all, you wouldn't think it so darn funny and, besides, maybe they don't have vulgar things like that in Oxford.'

'Maybe not, I never thought of asking. Anyway, I'm glad you finally decided to telephone instead because now you can bring me up to date with all the news. Where are you, by the way?'

'Still in Bath. They've gone to look at the American Museum this morning, would you believe? Apparently, it has this planet's largest collection of nineteenth-century New England patchwork quilts. I don't know why anyone would want to travel three thousand miles to see that kind of thing and I know even less what it has to do with crime fiction. But that's Colin for you. Any excuse to keep everyone on the move.'

'Perhaps they used to read the works of Edgar Allan Poe aloud to each other at the sewing parties. Or perhaps his mother made one of the quilts. Apart from that, is everything jogging along in harmony?'

'Oh, I guess so.'

'Don't you know?'

'All I know for sure is I'll be thankful when this is over and we can all go home. There seems to be some kind of jinx at work.'

I waited for her to elaborate and she said defensively: 'No need for that prim look I can hear on your face. It wasn't my responsibility this time. If anyone was to blame, it was Marilou.'

'Has something happened to Mrs Dearing?'

'She had an accident. Nothing serious and she wasn't hurt, but it shook her up. She was threatening to catch a plane back to Missouri, but we managed to talk her out of that.'

'What happened to her?'

'It was the morning we left to come here. We had to be downstairs at eight o'clock, when the bus was due to collect us. Most of us, including me, believe it or not, weren't more than five minutes late, but by twenty after there still wasn't any sign of Edith or Marilou and when Colin, who's our tour operator, tried to call their rooms there was no answer from either of them. Then eventually Marilou came down by the stairs. She told us her aunt had had a bad night, which had meant a late start and, on top of that, when they reached the elevators they'd waited all of ten minutes for one that wasn't already so crammed with passengers that there was no room for the wheelchair. No big surprise. They had the worst elevator service in that hotel that I ever came across anywhere in the world, including the one we're in now, which must rate pretty low. So, anyway, Marilou had been sent down to explain and to bring the elevator up to collect Edith.'

'Is that all?'

'No, only the background, so you'll understand. Marilou took an elevator up, as instructed. She was gone a hell of a long time and it turned out to be a case of shutting the stable door when the horse was halfway inside.'

'What can you be talking about?'

'Oh, I don't know, but you once said that Edith reminded you of a benevolent horse and it just came into my head. Apparently, an empty one had stopped right where she was waiting and she rolled her chair forward, like she often does, only this time something went wrong. She was half in, half out, and she found she couldn't move forward or back. Next thing was the doors closed on her like pincers and she was jammed up between them until someone finally came along and pulled her out.'

'Poor old lady, how very disagreeable!'

'Yes, Marilou said there was quite a crowd collected by the time she showed up, and someone had gone to get hold of a doctor. They were scared she was having a heart attack.'

'But it was a false alarm, I hope?'

'Well, I'm not too sure about that. She certainly wasn't in any fit state to travel. Finally, the rest of us went ahead in the bus and Edith and Marilou came down by car in the afternoon.'

'With Basil?'

'How did you know?'

'The voice of experience. Of your methods, I mean.'

'Well, I knew he'd take good care of her and it was something constructive I could do, instead of just standing around and wringing my hands. But you can understand why I have this feeling there's a jinx on us?'

'On the other hand, try not to become neurotic about it. After all, Edith brought it on herself. The silly old bird should never have tried a dodge like that in a strange hotel, especially one like the New Westminster which had obviously scarcely got the roof on when it opened its doors. She ought to have known better at her age.'

Amazingly enough, this announcement was greeted by a wail of distress:

'For God's sake, Tessa, don't *say* things like that.'

'Why not?'

'Because it's what she said herself and it's not true. She's not a silly old bird and you know it. She didn't believe it, even when she was saying it. Oh, can't you see what I'm driving at?'

'I'm not sure that I can.'

'Then you must be slipping.'

'Let me try again. How about this? I have an idea I know what you're talking about, but I hope it's the wrong one.'

'Too bad! Are you there, Tessa? What's the matter? Have you hung up on me, or something?'

'I was digesting your words.'

'Well, how was I expected to know that?'

'You might have been prepared for it. Anyway, here's something for you to think about in return. It may take you a while, but I'll be here for another couple of hours so call me back when you've got the answer, preferably before they all get back from the quilt show.'

'What's the question?'

'Cast your mind back. Recreate the scene in you head exactly as it was at the point, let's say, just before Marilou came down until the moment when she went up again. Three or four minutes, I imagine?'

'Doesn't sound difficult, I know, but it will be. We weren't the only tour staying in that hotel, for a start. There was a huge party moving out at just around the same time as we were. That's what caused the elevators being jammed up even worse than usual. There were people and luggage piled up all over the place.'

'Even so, surely your group would have stuck more or less together? How many others are there, by the way, apart from those I've met?'

'Only five. Two elderly women, they're friends, but they could be sisters. Both widows and they live in Florida. One's called Mrs Archibald, I forget the other.'

'That leaves three.'

'Yes, a Canadian family called McGowan. Middle-aged

couple with a daughter who's just graduated. Someone told me this trip was her reward for coming out top of her class, or whatever.'

'But those five are in a different league from your lot?'

'Yes, no bad feelings, as far as I know, although I have an idea Cornelius started by making a pass at the daughter and got warned off by Dad. But the real answer is that we just seemed to fall naturally into two separate groups. You know how that can happen in this kind of artificial instant-togetherness?'

'All the same, you may as well include them in your reconstruction.'

'OK, I'll try.'

'And don't worry too much about it. It will most likely turn out to be unnecessary and irrelevant and, even if it did provide a clue of some sort, there'd be nothing much either of us could do about it.'

'No, but it might help to prevent this joker trying it again.'

'How right you are!' I told her. 'One should always think positive.'

As usual, it was Mrs Parkes who answered the telephone, but this time, instead of cutting out the middleman, I asked to speak to Toby in person.

'It's about his tickets for tonight,' I explained. 'Nothing desperate, but I can't remember whether it was two or three he wanted and the box-office is getting jumpy about it. No trouble with yours, though. I've got you two in the front row of the dress circle for the late show on Saturday. Right?'

'Oh, I expect that'll do fairly well, thank you. So long as he's got enough leg room.'

Since she must have known as well as I did that Mr Parkes's legs measured approximately twelve inches from thigh to ankle, I considered this to be taking caution to unnecessary lengths, but the truth is that Mrs Parkes would never pass up the most fragile opportunity to demonstrate her contempt for any play I happened to be appearing in. However, I do not take umbrage because Toby has explained that this is only because she has my welfare at heart and does not wish me to spoil my chances by getting above myself.

'Hold on a minute,' she commanded, having served this ace, 'and I'll see what I can do.'

Toby kept me waiting for not more than six or seven minutes, at the end of which I said:

'I've forgotten whether you want two or three for tonight.'

'What nonsense! I told you only the day before yesterday that Macintosh and I would be coming together and you said that would suit you well because we could take you out to supper afterwards and he'd be able to tell you the local gossip. You'll have to do better than that.'

'Oh yes, sorry. You must put it down to first-night nerves.'

'No, that won't do either, so stop wasting my valuable time and tell me what you've really rung up for.'

'Well, the fact is, Toby, I didn't particularly want to go into all this in front of Dr Macintosh, but I wondered if you'd do me a big favour and invite Mervyn Houghton to lunch on Sunday?'

'I'm not surprised it took you so long to come to the point. What a revolting idea!'

'I know, but there's something I want to try and find out from him and I rather want Robin to meet him too.'

'Oh, very well, I'll see what I can do. He may not come, though.'

'Whyever not? Since when has he been known to turn down the offer of a free lunch?'

'It's a new departure, I agree, but rumours abound that he is becoming rather reclusive these days.'

'Probably forced on him by the fact that he doesn't get invited any more. He'll be all the more keen.'

'Yes, well, if you insist. I don't suppose you intend to tell me what's behind this sudden urge to see him?'

'Well, it's quite a long story, Toby, and . . .'

'In that case, don't bother. I don't wish to spend my whole

morning talking about Mervyn and it probably wouldn't be true, anyway, so there's nothing to be gained.'

Lorraine called back within the hour, full of apologies and remorse:

'It's no good, Tessa, you picked the wrong Watson this time. I'm not cut out for the sleuthing job.'

'Can't you remember anything at all about who was present and who not?'

'I have some vague notions, but nothing exact.'

'Vague notions will be better than none. Who do they apply to?'

'Well, Ed for one.'

'OK, so start with him.'

'You remember the layout of that hotel? All that open space made it harder than ever to keep track of people. They could just kind of wander off and disappear from sight and then materialise again and you wouldn't have any idea how long they'd been away. All I do remember about Ed, though, was that he wasn't with us when Marilou came downstairs because I was standing close to Virginia and she had been complaining about the delay and everything and also what an age Ed was taking. So I said I hoped we hadn't lost him now, as well as Edith, or something stupid like that.'

'And what did Virginia say?'

'That he'd only gone to the drugstore to get her some toothpaste because she might have left hers in the bathroom and they'd handed in their key. It shouldn't have taken him more than five minutes.'

'And how long did it take him?'

'Well, that's where I fall down because, like I told you, it was around then that Marilou arrived and started to explain about Edith and I was concentrating on her. I can't tell you when Ed came back.'

'Never mind, try some of the others.'

'Cornelius is next and he was even worse. Half the time he

was with us and the other half he wasn't. You know how he is? Can't remain on the same spot for an instant and he seemed to bounce up beside you at one minute, with some joke or other, which wasn't particularly funny, and before you could answer he would have bounced off again. I do recall one time, though, when he must have been gone longer than usual because his wife sent Colin off to find him and bring him back. She's always handing out orders like that and I don't know how he stands for it.'

'Yes, I noticed she had a somewhat imperious manner. Anyone else on your list?'

'Well, yes, I guess so,' she replied, with so much reluctance that I could tell what was coming.

'Beverly, I suppose?'

'Right, but listen, Tessa, it doesn't have to mean anything. She's another grasshopper who can't stay in the same place for two minutes in a row.'

'I realise that and I daresay nothing will come of this, anyway. I just thought it would be worth while trying to find out which of them might have had the opportunity to play that nasty trick on Mrs Dearing. Where did Beverly hop to on this occasion?'

'The third floor.'

'Oh, you mean she went up in the lift with Marilou? Well, fine! That must be about the best alibi anyone could have.'

'Oh, sure. The trouble is she doesn't have it. She could have been there several minutes ahead of Marilou. She went up by the stairs.'

'Whatever for?'

'Don't you ever listen to me? That's the way she is these days. When Marilou started explaining what had happened, Bev didn't wait for her to finish. She just gave one of those wild squeaks and called out something about how poor darling Mrs Dearing must be feeling so awful, all alone up there, and off she galloped.'

'And was she still keeping the poor old lady company when Marilou returned?'

'No, she wasn't.'

'Honestly, Lorraine, getting blood out of a stone would be child's play compared to this. Why wasn't she?'

'Lost her way, landed up on the wrong floor and went searching up and down the wrong corridors. You have to admit it's a mistake anyone could have made.'

'Do I?'

'It's this quaint way you have here of calling the second floor the first and so on, up to the top. It's all done to confuse the unwary foreigner and it always works.'

'Yes, I hadn't thought of that. So what happened next? Did she eventually find her way back to what we quaintly call the ground floor?'

'It took a while. First Colin, who'd gone up to investigate by this time, brought back the news that Edith wasn't feeling too well and had gone to her room to rest. He was going to lay on a car to bring her and Marilou to Bath during the afternoon. That's when I asked him to let me handle that end of it because I knew just the right man for the job. We weren't out of the wood yet, though, because when I came back, after making my call to Basil, there they were, all still waiting for Beverly. That's when I was afraid Colin really would start throwing things. Normally, he's so calm and patient, but this had really broken his nerve and when Cornelius offered to go looking for Beverly himself, it was just about the last straw. Luckily, Mrs Neilsen realised he was about to explode and told Cornelius to stay right where he was. Not long after that Beverly finally appeared, so we were able to straggle on to the bus not much over an hour late, without anyone getting murdered. None of which has been much help, I guess?'

'Except that, as you said, it may help to prevent any future disaster. You'd better keep a sharp watch on Beverly's comings and goings, plus an eye on Cornelius and Ed as well, if you can manage all that without squinting. Any idea why one of those three should want to play such a nasty trick?'

Lorraine turned silent again and I repeated the question.

'I heard you, Tessa, and the answer has to be yes.'

'Which one?'

'All three.'

'Are you serious? Well, of course you are, it's hardly a thing to joke about. So start with Beverly. What grudge could she conceivably have against the poor harmless old lady?'

'Perhaps not quite so harmless as she appears. She's certainly very observant and shrewd. However, the point is that everyone has been treating Beverly with kid gloves all these months while she was getting better, so scared she might have a relapse if she was crossed. She's grown unaccustomed to being snubbed or put down.'

'And Mrs Dearing has broken this pattern, has she?'

'I don't mean she's unkind. She just treats Beverly like you would any girl who was monopolising the conversation and I have the feeling that Bev doesn't care for it.'

'I can see that she wouldn't. How about Cornelius? Does Edith put him down too?'

'Sure, all the time, and it's water off a duck's back. The only way you could put Cornelius down would be with a poleaxe. No, in his case there wouldn't be any malice in it, it's just that he has a weird sense of humour, the kind of man who would creep up behind you in the street and stick the sharp end of an umbrella in your back.'

'And go laughing merrily on his way if you dropped dead with a heart attack?'

'Oh, you bet. And his wife would growl: "How careless you are, Cornelius. Look what you have done now!"'

'Yes, theirs is an odd sort of relationship, isn't it? Still, back to our list. I suppose we can virtually rule out Ed, can't we? Can't we?' I repeated as the line went silent again.

'Maybe not entirely.'

'What? A fine, upstanding all-American boy like Ed?'

'Yes, that's how he seems, but there's something you don't

know about him. There wasn't any reason why you should and, aside from that, the two or three people who do know have spent the last two-and-a-half years trying to forget it. You'd better have it now, though. Twenty-four hours before their wedding he stood Virginia up.'

'How'd he do that?'

'Walked out. Jilted her.'

'And here's me thinking they were married.'

'So they are, but it was touch and go. What Robin would call a close-run thing.'

'It sounds enthralling. Tell me.'

'It was the day before the wedding. Virginia was at home with her parents, of course, and Ed was supposed to drive up that morning and spend the night with some friends of theirs in the neighbourhood. At around lunchtime his hostess called Lynn to say he hadn't turned up. She was a bit bothered because she had invited one or two other girls and boys and the plan was that after lunch they'd all swim and play tennis. She was calling to find out if there'd been some misunderstanding. Lynn said no, she didn't know what could have held him up. She was worried stiff, though, convinced that Ed had been involved in some automobile accident and she asked her friend to call again the minute she had any news of him. She didn't mention a word about it in front of Virginia, but as soon as she could get Earl on his own she told him.'

'And what was Earl's reaction?'

'He took it badly. It was curious because it's supposed to be women who have the intuition, and there was Lynn worried about car crashes, whereas the first thing Earl said was that he'd had a foreboding for days now that something like this would happen. He just wished the damned idiot hadn't left it till the last minute, otherwise they'd have had a chance to sort it out.'

'Had he run off with someone else?'

'No, just got cold feet and the feeling he couldn't go through with it. I guess a lot of grooms get to feel like that just hours before the knot is tied, don't you?'

'Practically all of them, I should imagine, but the vast

majority get even colder feet at the thought of backing out.'

'Well, Ed didn't. He'd gone to any amount of trouble to hide himself away where they wouldn't find him until it was too late and all the arrangements had been cancelled.'

'Although they did find him and dragged him back, presumably?'

'Yes, that's how Henry came to be involved. Being a lawyer, he has contacts with all kinds of strange people, the sort of people you and I hardly know exist. It took about six hours to flush Ed out. I don't know what bribery or threats they used, but whatever it was it worked. There must have been nearly a thousand guests at that wedding, but I'll bet you not more than half a dozen of them ever knew how close it had come to being called off. They certainly wouldn't have guessed.'

'Was Virginia told?'

'No. Ed may have confessed afterwards, but I doubt it. Beverly doesn't know either.'

'Well, it's a sad story, but they seem perfectly pleased with each other now, so perhaps it was all for the best. And, honestly, Lorraine, I don't see that it has much bearing. It may show Ed and a few other people up in rather a poor light, but that's quite a different matter from playing a malicious trick on a harmless old woman.'

'Maybe, but most of us who know the whole story believe it was the shock and worry of those last twenty-four hours which brought on Earl's heart attack. I know that's how Lynn feels and she's never going to forgive Ed for it.'

'Yes, but, as I keep saying, that's different. It can't have been his intention.'

'No, but it could have given him ideas afterwards, because, you know what, Tessa? Another one who's liable to drop dead with a heart attack, given the right circumstances, is Edith Dearing.'

9

Various factors had contributed to making Mervyn Houghton one of the richest as well as most unpopular men in the neighbourhood. The first, from which most of the others derived, was that he had never known his father, who had been killed in Normandy during the Allied invasion of Europe when Mervyn, his only child, was two years old, thereby pre-deceasing his own father and wiping out a whole generation of death duties. A few years later the father had followed him to the grave, as the result of coming a cropper in the hunting field, at which point the title and property had passed to Mervyn, the latter doubling and redoubling in value during the remaining years of his minority.

His mother, now in her seventies, had never remarried, thus creating another serious impediment to his acquiring emotional maturity, far less a sense of humour or humility. She was an arrogant, obtuse woman, with a great deal of money in her own right, to compensate for an indifferent education and a mind which, to all intents and purposes, had shut up shop at the age of nineteen when she had married into the gentry and become the chatelaine of Warne Hill.

Endowed with splendid health and boundless energy, she had spent most of her widowhood hectoring anyone who came near enough to hear her and interfering in the lives of her neigh-bours and the tenants on the three-thousand-acre estate. Her principal mission in life, however, had been to instil into her son the belief that he was a favoured member of a superior breed, that these advantages carried no matching obligations or responsibilities, and that his first duty in life was to hold on tight to everything he'd got.

Mervyn was an apt pupil and now, in middle age, when he claimed, as he was sometimes heard to, that his best friend was his mother, there were few who felt disposed to argue.

She certainly had no rival in Toby and, watching them together, I marvelled that two men of approximately the same age, both bachelors, however temporarily in Toby's case, who had been to the same sort of school and lived within twenty miles of each other, should be such poles apart in all the important aspects.

Pursuing this theme, I had mentally drifted away, trying without success to think of a comparable paradox between two females, and so failed to take in the question Mervyn had evidently just flung in my direction; the natural tendency to do this being exacerbated by his bulging pale-blue eyes, huge stomach and rosebud mouth, with pinkish hair sprouting around it, all making it painful to look straight at him.

'Sorry, Mervyn, what did you say?'

'Just asked if you were still treading the boards these days?'

Robin, who becomes incensed with rage at the merest hint of my being under attack from anyone but himself, answered for me:

'Not only treading them, her footsteps are reverberating throughout the land. She has just finished a film, is about to star in a new television serial and is at present leading a distinguished cast in a play at Oxford.'

'Oh, really? Must try and take my mama over to see it one evening.'

'I doubt if that will be possible,' I told him. 'It's only on for a limited season and they tell me it's booked solid for every performance.'

This was slightly wide of the truth, but his patronising

76

attitude always brings out the childish streak in me and also it was the best means I could think of, on the spur of the moment, to ward off the inevitable request for free tickets.

'You surprise me, but I suppose it's only on at the small theatre, isn't it? And the university's probably still up?'

'Yes, it is, although I don't think that carries any weight. We don't get much gown in the audience, or much town either, come to that. It's mainly the tourist trade we live by.'

'Well, well! I wouldn't have thought all the coachloads of gawpers had much time for our little home-grown provincial theatres.'

'Not all do, I daresay, but there are some very up-market American tours doing the rounds these days. There's a party over here at the moment, for instance. . . . Oh, my goodness, what an amazing coincidence!' I added, taking care not to overdo the thunderstruck act.

This may have been a misjudgement, however, for Mervyn evinced no curiosity whatsoever. Instead, he pulled out a crumpled package of miniature black cheroots, a taste I felt sure he had cultivated to enable himself to smoke as much as he pleased, without the risk of anyone cadging one off him.

Having lighted up, he puffed out a great cloud of foul-smelling smoke, threw the spent match on the table, missing the ashtray by inches, and addressed himself to Toby:

'Seen anything of those friends of yours, the Dalrymples, lately?'

'Not very lately, which is hardly surprising. They have moved to Northumberland or Arizona, or somewhere. What was your amazing coincidence, Tessa?'

'Didn't you tell me that the woman who was murdered here last weekend had some connection with the overseas tourist trade?'

'Yes, so I did! Matthews told me she was working for some American magazine which deals with that kind of thing. There now!'

'I suppose you know all about that sensation, Mervyn?'

77

'Good bit more than you do, I shouldn't wonder. Her name was Barbara Landauer and she had an appointment to see me at four o'clock that afternoon. Didn't turn up, needless to say.'

'Well, I never! That's an even more amazing coincidence. What did she want to see you about?'

'Just background information, I gather, for some article she was writing on English manor houses. As it happens, she wouldn't have seen me, even if she had stayed alive long enough.'

'Oh, why not?'

'The Haig-Robinsons had invited me over for lunch at their place. They had a chap coming down who'd been working on a study of a particularly rare species of butterfly which only survives in a small area of Peru and I wasn't going to pass that up. Not that one had much chance to discuss anything interesting, with my host going on about his new gold-plated helicopter, or some such ostentation. Still, I did manage to arrange matters so that I could drive Hollins to Storhampton for his train back to London, when I got him to expand a bit on the subject.'

'So perhaps, as it turned out, it was just as well that Mrs Landauer was unable to keep her appointment with you?'

'Wouldn't have mattered. I'd laid on my head keeper to show her round and my mama was going to give her a dish of tea. Between them, they know a good deal more about the history and running of the place than I do. Tell me, Price, what do you think of this footling idea I was reading about the other day of doing away with JPs and handing the whole caboodle over to magistrates' courts?'

'It is hardly my province,' Robin replied, 'but it's possible that there are one or two shortcomings in the present system which could do with tidying up.'

'Oh, you think so, do you? Then just listen to this. My mother has been a JP for over forty years and there's not much about the system, or the kind of wrong 'un it deals with, that she doesn't know. It is her considered opinion and she's no fool, believe me. . . .'

He boomed on in this strain for at least five minutes and, although I could not applaud his methods, they did effectively banish the subject of Mrs Landauer's murder for that afternoon. Any attempt on my part to reintroduce it would have made me sound as boorish as himself and would probably have been doomed to failure, in any case.

However, I was not totally discouraged. To have gone to such trouble to bluster his way into this new topic, and thereby drive his host and fellow guests into torpors of boredom, must indicate that the old one held pitfalls for him which he was uncertain of being able to sidestep.

'You could be right, I suppose,' Robin conceded, when Mervyn had finally marched away on the fullest of stomachs and Toby had retired, exhausted, to his own quarters, 'but I shouldn't try to wring too much significance from it, if I were you.'

'Why not? You must have noticed how he grabbed at the first straw to shy off the subject of Barbara Landauer?'

'Naturally I did, but it doesn't follow that he was afraid of betraying himself. It is much more likely that, now the woman has ceased to be a potential source of revenue, he has simply lost interest in her. Furthermore . . .'

'What?'

'If there had been anything bogus in that story of what he was up to last Sunday afternoon, you may be sure Matthews would have ferreted it out by now.'

'You mean the luncheon party for the man from Peru?'

'Exactly, and driving the man from Peru to the station afterwards. Checking it out with the hosts would have been a simple matter of routine.'

'He may not know much about the Haig-Robinsons, though. They haven't been here very long.'

'What's that got to do with it?'

'Well, you know how stick-in-the-mud most people are round here. It's not only snobbishness, it's just that they tend to regard all newcomers with suspicion, whoever they are. It takes

79

ages to get accepted and the Haig-Robinsons have worked much too hard at it, which has merely slowed down the process.'

'Houghton seems to have accepted them without too much trouble.'

'Well, he would, wouldn't he? They're extremely rich and extremely hospitable. That's another thing that puts people off.'

'Quite hard to please, apparently. Which do they object to most? The money or the hospitality?'

'Oh, you know what I mean, Robin. This couple are so desperately lavish and pretentious. Three wineglasses at every place-setting and enough silver to sink a battleship. Ordinary people hesitate to invite them back because they feel they can't compete. So, in order not to be compelled to invite them back, they don't accept their invitations. It's a vicious circle, but naturally it doesn't apply to Mervyn. For one thing he knows, and they know too, that if he ever did bring out his own silver it would make theirs look silly and, furthermore, I don't suppose the necessity to invite them back has ever crossed his mind.'

'So what this all adds up to, I gather, is that in your opinion the Haig-Robinsons would provide him with a false alibi any day of the week, sooner than lose their one and only friend?'

'No, I'm sure they wouldn't go as far as that, certainly not deliberately. What I can envisage, though, at some point in the afternoon, is Mervyn jumping up and saying: "Oh, my goodness, four o'clock already. I'd no idea I'd stayed so long" and walking out without more ado. They'd feel rather sheepish trying to detain him by pointing out that it was only three. You can get away with a lot, you know, if you're bumptious and autocratic enough.'

'Though not with murder, we hope. Where do these people live?'

'The Haig-Robinsons? Oh, only just up the road towards Dedley. Four or five miles away, roughly.'

'I see.'

I did not enquire whether he intended to tip Sergeant Matthews off, for fear that he would either give me a false answer, or say that he would need to think it over before deciding. However, I saw no reason why that should deter me from making a few enquiries of my own and, when he had dropped me at my place of lodging on Monday morning, I spent half an hour experimenting with different-coloured eyeshadow, while considering ways and means of putting the plan into operation.

10

There was no message from Lorraine when I returned from a shopping expedition a few hours later, but the tour bus must have arrived in Oxford on schedule because she turned up punctually at one o'clock for our rendezvous at Casa Oliviera.

'Thanks for the flowers,' she said, giving me a powerful hug. 'They're gorgeous and so are you. They must have cost you two weeks' salary.'

'Not so. I pinched them at sunrise from Toby's garden.'

'And that vase they're in? I bet that's not hotel property?'

'No, that's on loan, as I should have explained in my note. I brought a small one along as well, while I was about it, and stuck some lavender in it for Mrs Dearing. I thought it might appeal to her.'

'You were right. She was so touched she almost wept, and she was dictating her thank-you letter to Marilou before the poor creature even had time to unpack her bags. Just wait till I tell her you took all that trouble to arrange them yourself.'

'No trouble. This is the most casual, free-and-easy hotel I've ever stayed in. They seem to hand over people's keys to anyone, on demand. Still, it has one big advantage which we ought to be thankful for.'

'What's that?'

'The lift. As you may have noticed, it's one of those old-fashioned iron cages that need two strong men to open and shut. At least there's no danger of the hanky-panky that went on in London. I trust there hasn't been any repetition of it, by the way?'

'Well . . . no, there hasn't.'

'No upsets of any kind, in fact?'

'Can't think of any.'

'And, no doubt, you'd remember if there had been. What's everyone doing now?'

'Having lunch at one of the colleges. It could be the one Appleby went to, but I'm not too sure of that.'

'You don't sound sure of anything this morning, Lorraine.'

'Oh, I do too. What an idea.'

'OK, have it your own way. What happens this afternoon?'

'They take a walk in the botanical gardens, then up through some meadow, after which Colin turns them loose in the bookstore, which is the moment most of them have been waiting for. All except Edith, that is.'

'Who's not so keen?'

'She says the wheelchair would only be a nuisance to everyone, but I think the truth is that the bus ride this morning tired her out more than she will admit.'

'And what will you be doing this afternoon?'

'Haven't decided. Maybe I'll sit with Edith for a while. Marilou has been given a list of books as long as your arm, so the old lady will be on her own for once and I just discovered something about her which makes me curious, only I won't be able to tell her what it is. Want to hear?'

'I might die of frustration if I didn't.'

'Edith Dearing is her married name. She was better known as Edith Mae McClintock.'

'Good heavens, I thought she'd died years ago.'

'So did a lot of people, I guess, if they were old enough to have heard the name.'

'Well, I must say, you do surprise me. I haven't read any McClintock novels for years, but I used to adore them when I was a child, mainly because they were so soppy and romantic. I know they ranked as crime novels, but there was such a lot of old-fashioned true romance thrown in and somehow I don't associate Edith Dearing with that sort of stuff.'

83

'All the same, I could see how, if you found you could churn it out and people would snap it up, it would be an easy way of making a hell of a lot of money.'

'Yes, I suppose so. Did she tell you herself?'

'No, Colin did.'

'Oh yes, your faithful sheepdog. And she told him, did she?'

'No, I'd say it was more likely he put two and two together. She talks to him a lot and he doesn't miss a trick. But he said, whatever else, I shouldn't mention it to her, or tell any of the others because it might embarrass her.'

'I hope you feel flattered?'

'What about?'

'That he recognised that you could be relied upon to keep it to yourself.'

'Oh no, Tessa, all it means is that he recognises me as an outsider. He caught on right away that I wasn't a true, dedicated crime-story fan and clearly, in some ways, that makes a welcome change. He guessed I'd be amused, but not all that deeply impressed, and I wouldn't be tempted to go blabbing about it to the others. I only passed it on to you because I thought you'd be amused, too, and you do so love to find out every tiny thing about each new person you meet.'

'Yes, how true, and I'm grateful and also relieved that your report is so innocuous, for once. No sinister or disturbing features at all, by the sound of it.'

Lorraine had become so engrossed in the business of snatching the bill from the waitress before I could get my hands on it, then asking what tip she should leave and doubling the amount suggested, that the last question had apparently fallen on deaf ears. However, on the way back to the hotel she said:

'As it happens, Tessa, there has been one other development.'

'But nothing sinister or disturbing, I trust?'

'No, I'd say on the whole it was good news. Apparently, Beverly has lost the very special camera Earl gave her just before he died.'

'Yes, I know that. What's so good about it?'

'Well, I'll be . . . The first time I heard about it was last night and the good news is that it has turned up again. The only worrying part is all the lies she told about it.'

'Oh yes, like what?'

'Well, I'd missed out on all this, but apparently Virginia noticed right away that she didn't have it with her and Beverly told her it had jammed and she'd taken it to a shop to be repaired. Only, yesterday Virginia sneaked a look inside that great bag of hers she carries around all the time and there was the camera.'

'Which caused those eyebrows to be raised even higher, I daresay?'

'Because there certainly hadn't been time for the shop to mail it to her. So that's when the full story came out. She hadn't dared tell Virginia she'd lost it because there'd be an awful scene and she just couldn't take it. But then, when it turned up again, she hadn't dared mention that either because she'd have been accused of lying in the first place. Poor kid, she was in tears by the time she'd finished explaining it all, but did you ever hear of anything more stupid and unnecessary in your life?'

'No, never.'

'I know Virginia can be uppity sometimes, especially since she achieved the status of married woman, and she's certainly ready to tell everyone what's good for them, but she's not a gorgon. Honestly, Tess, it makes me wonder, you know.'

'Wonder what?'

'Whether those shrinks had got it right and it *was* such a good idea to bring her on this trip. It's this trick she has of saying just anything that comes into her head to get herself out of trouble which has me worried. Now tell me I'm over-reacting and making mountains out of molehills?'

'No,' I confessed, 'I can't this time. In fact, Lorraine, in my opinion you may have rather more to worry about than you realise.'

(2)

A tall, sandy-haired man, aged somewhere between thirty-five and forty and wearing a tweed suit which had seen better days, was standing beside the reception desk when we walked into the hotel.

He was checking his watch with the clock behind the desk and, falling automatically into my habit of inventing an instant biography for every passing stranger, I set him down as one who hoped his wife would be punctual for once, so that they could get home in time to take the dogs for a walk before tea.

However, on catching sight of Lorraine, he gave the lie to this by advancing towards her with both arms outstretched.

'Hi, Colin!' she said.

'Hi there, Lorraine, what a bit of luck. I was hovering here in the hope of running into you.'

'And just look what else you've run into. You haven't met Tessa yet, have you? Colin Gascoine, Theresa Crichton.'

'No, although I've seen you many times from afar,' he said, shaking hands and smiling, and then he launched into the ever acceptable patter about what a thrill it was to meet me, how much he looked forward to seeing the play, which the whole of Oxford seemed to be raving about, and how his daughter would never forgive him if he went home without my autograph.

For once, though, I scarcely listened. All the while he was rattling on I was recalling with amusement Toby's self-confessed inability to recognise the person behind the veneer and thinking that I could beat him at that game any day of the week.

It was true that the picture I had formed of Colin was based solely on hearsay, and only snippets at that, but the deferential, anxious young man of my imagination, with a light build, well adapted to running about at top speed and wearing a dark suit to distinguish him from the customers, could hardly have been wider of the mark.

'Thank you very much,' I said, when he had made his point, 'I am most flattered. You're English, aren't you?'

''Fraid so. Any objection?'

'Of course he's English,' Lorraine said. 'What else, for

goodness sake? You don't imagine they'd hire a Frenchman or a Chinese to take us around these places, do you? Listen, Colin, is there something you want to see me about? If so, why don't we all go and sit down in that morgue they call the coffee room? I've never seen anyone in there, so the chances are we'll have it to ourselves.'

'No, no, Lorraine, certainly not. I wouldn't dream of dragging you away from Miss Crichton. It can wait.'

'You won't be dragging me away from her. I don't imagine this is a personal matter and, even if it is, it wouldn't matter Tessa hearing. We tell each other everything.'

Colin showed some surprise at hearing this, but I like to think I was more successful in concealing my own. I was not displeased either. It suited me well to be present during their talk, not so much from curiosity as from the hope that it would help to put me on the same footing with Colin as the members of his team, thereby making it easier, when the chance came, to elicit some information on quite a different subject.

'Over there suit you?' he enquired, pointing to a table and some armchairs by a window.

'Looks fine to me,' Lorraine agreed, heading towards them.

As she had so nearly predicted, the room had only two other occupants, both seated too far away to be within earshot, although both had looked up quickly, and then away again, as we entered.

'Something tells me they are hoping to order some coffee,' Colin remarked, 'and something else tells me they are going to be disappointed. If you'll both excuse me for a moment, I'll go and organise things at source.'

'Isn't he great?' Lorraine asked, watching him saunter away.

'Oh yes, and, having met him, I'm more convinced than ever that he has a slight crush on you.'

'Well, to be honest with you, Tessa, I do believe there was a little misunderstanding there, right at the start, but he's what you and Robin would call the perfect gent. Soon as he realised I

87

was happily married, there was never any more trouble.'

'How sad for him, though. Several romances seem to have been nipped in the bud already on this trip.'

'Why do you say that?'

'Didn't you tell me Cornelius had made a pass at the Canadian girl and got his comeuppance from Dad?'

'Oh, Cornelius! He's in quite a different category. He'd make a pass at anyone over the age of twelve. Colin's not like that. He just goes out of his way to make everyone feel special. He was like that with Beverly at the start. I guess he saw at once that she needed attention and reassurance and wasn't getting much of it from her sister. But he backed down at once when he realised there was a danger she would take him too seriously. And he's a miracle of efficiency, as well as sensitive and kind. You could drop dead in this hotel and it would be months before anyone noticed, but Colin has only to lift a finger and they all come running. You wait and see.'

He was as good as her word, returning in under five minutes, followed by an elderly and lugubrious waiter wearing a martyred expression, as though wondering what on earth he would be required to do next.

'It is not exactly personal,' Colin said, as Lorraine handed him some coffee, 'but rather a tricky situation has developed and I need your help.'

'That doesn't sound too promising. It's lucky we have Tessa here. Handing out advice is second nature to her. What's it all about?'

'Beverly, I'm afraid.'

'Oh no, don't tell me she's in trouble again?'

'I must, unfortunately. That's why I want to consult you before taking any action. You dropped me a hint, right at the start, that she might need rather careful handling and I'm ashamed to say that I didn't take it seriously enough. I noticed, of course, that she was apt to be somewhat high-pitched and on edge sometimes, but I put it down to a combination of high spirits and the ingrained habit of taking the mickey out of that solemn Virginia, whenever she got the chance.'

'So what's she done now? And where is she, by the way?'

'With Edith. Marilou's been turned loose with a list of books as long as your arm, so it seemed a sensible arrangement. I can rely on the old lady not to stand any nonsense, or to let Beverly out of her sight until the others get back.'

'But why isn't she still with them at the bookstore?'

'She escaped; that's what I have to explain. That is, if you're still sure you want Miss Crichton to be dragged in?'

'Oh, sure, don't worry about Tessa. How do you mean, she escaped?'

'It was about an hour ago. I brought Edith back here and when I'd made her comfortable and ordered her tea I went back to check on the rest of my flock. They all seemed quite happy, no problems for once. Some of them said they were going to spend a little more time browsing and one or two wanted to find a bank or do a bit of shopping in the department store across the road, but they all knew about the schedule and promised to be back and ready to leave for Banbury at five. When I say all . . .'

'You don't include Beverly?'

'I was assured by Helen Neilsen that she was down in the basement, helping Ed and Virginia to find some books on sailing. Helen's so totally reliable, as a rule, that I took her word for it. The truth is, I'm afraid that there was an item of shopping I had in mind for myself. It's my wife's birthday next week and they have some very fancy cashmeres at that shop, so I left them to manage on their own for half an hour.'

'And why the hell not? They're supposed to be adults, not a bunch of schoolkids.'

'Unfortunately not everyone behaves in an adult way when they're in a strange environment and the fact is that, if you wanted to be pernickety, you could say that I was using the firm's time to pursue my private ends. That's why I'm hoping to keep this business hushed up as far as possible. It shouldn't be too difficult because I don't forsee Beverly, who is the only other person involved, being in any hurry to give me away. She was already in the shop when I got there, I should explain. I hadn't noticed her, but her presence was brought to my attention in a somewhat disagreeable way.'

Lorraine's response to this was such a long and heartfelt groan that one of the other people in the room lowered his newspaper long enough to give her a glare of disapproval.

'I'm not going to like this, I can tell.'

'All the same, please hear me out. I was trying to choose between two cardigans for my wife when I became aware of some kind of hubbub going on just a few yards from the counter. I don't know if you've been inside that shop, but it's designed so that each department merges into the adjoining one, without any clear-cut division. This fracas seemed to be taking place among the women's underwear, where I could see half a dozen people clustered round the cash desk and, above all the other noises, a female voice, squeaking and wailing, which was familiar enough to send shivers down a stiffer spine than mine.'

'What mess had she got herself into this time?'

'Being arrested for shoplifting, no less.'

'Oh, my God, Colin!'

'Exactly!'

'I just can't believe she'd do a thing like that. What is she supposed to have stolen?'

'A satin and lace nightgown. It was priced at over forty pounds.'

'There must have been some lunatic mistake. Apart from everything else, she doesn't wear lace and satin nightgowns. She goes to bed in a kind of track suit.'

'Alas, it appears that trifles of that kind are the last thing to bother the average shoplifter. There may be some mistake, of course, but her story was not terribly convincing. A child of six could have done better.'

'What was her story?' I asked, since Lorraine had now slumped back in her chair, apparently too distraught to put the question herself.

'That it must have been a plant,' Colin replied, looking at me as though surprised to find I was still there. 'It doesn't sound very probable.'

'Planted where? In her shopping bag?'

'Handbag, I suppose you'd call it. A whopping great thing, large enough to accommodate the infant Worthing. It goes wherever she goes, although quite often she is unable to remember where she has just put it down. She hadn't even bothered to tuck this garment out of sight, which is why one of the assistants noticed it as she was walking away. At that point anyone with a grain of sense would have tried the dodge of pretending that she had dumped it there while looking at some other bits and pieces, with the intention of taking the whole lot to the cash desk at one go. It might have been difficult to disprove, as I imagine it to be the kind of misunderstanding that does arise from time to time and she hadn't attempted to leave the premises. As it was, she got herself into a right old tangle.'

'But listen, Colin,' Lorraine said, coming to life again. 'You said just now that she was with Edith. Does that mean everything worked out OK in the end?'

'Oh, we got her off the hook, if that's what you mean. By a great stroke of luck, the floor supervisor who was called in to deal with it turned out to be an old acquaintance of mine from Merton days, when her father was landlord of the Three Bells. That was a help, but what really turned the scales was her American passport. Your compatriots account for about eighty per cent of the turnover just now and they wouldn't want to do anything to jeopardise that. However, the point I want to make, Lorraine, is that she may have got away with it this time, but how about the next and the one after that? Not wishing to be unkind, I'm coming to believe that she's not always fully responsible for her actions and, strictly speaking, is not in a fit state to be on a tour of this kind.'

'Oh well, I don't know, Colin . . . you mustn't be too hard on her. I know she's been through a bad time, but she has a clean bill of health now and this holiday was designed to set her up once and for all.'

'I daresay it was, but it's not doing much to set me up, I have to tell you. We had a close call this afternoon and, if the scales had tipped the other way, it's my reputation which would have suffered. Furthermore, Lorraine, and forgive me for saying this, but if you mean what I suspect you mean, I do think I should have been given advance warning. I can understand why her family wouldn't wish the facts to be generally known, but I think you could have relied on my discretion there and at least I'd have been prepared.'

'Yes, when you put it like that, maybe you have a point. I guess we were all so busy trying to protect Bev and build up her confidence that we didn't stop to consider anyone else. I'm sorry, though, and I'll do whatever I can to make amends. Just tell me how you suggest I should handle it.'

'You're not going to like it, but here goes. I want her to pack her bags and go home.'

'Oh no, Colin, you couldn't be so cruel. Imagine what it would do to her poor mother!'

'I'm afraid I can only see it from one point of view just now and I know what it will do to me, if she stays. It could end with my being thrown out of my job.'

'No, listen, please, Colin, I implore you. I'll do anything you say, short of that. I'll make sure she's never out of our sight for a single minute, but you can't ask us to send her home. If she's not fit to be here, she's damn well not fit to travel on her own, the state she'd be in. And it wouldn't be fair to expect Virginia and Ed to go with her. They've already cancelled one holiday they'd been saving for.'

'So what alternative does that leave?' he asked gently. 'Only one that I can see.'

'You mean me? You think I should take her?'

'I'm asking you to consider it. Sorry as I should be to lose you, Lorraine, there are a number of things I've learned about you during our short acquaintance. One is that you have a heart of gold and another is that by no stretch of the imagination could one say you were short of money. Perhaps most important of all, from my point of view, is that you're not a serious murder addict at all. It's quite obvious that you only came along for the ride and my suggestion is that it's a ride you could take any time you chose to.'

'Well, yes . . . that's true, I suppose, but listen, Colin. . . . Oh, I don't know, I don't know anything any more. What do you think I should do, Tessa?'

'I don't expect you to make up your mind here and now,' he cut in before I could reply, 'and, anyway, it's time to start rounding everyone up for Banbury. Think it over and perhaps we could have another chat this evening. Goodbye, Miss Crichton, and do forgive me. I'd been so looking forward to the chance of meeting you and I am truly sorry that it had to be in such unhappy circumstances.'

'Never mind, there are bound to be other occasions. What is there to see at Banbury, apart from a fine lady on a white horse?'

'There's also a haunted house not far away, which provided the setting for a celebrated novel of the thirties. It's a private house, but, as a special favour and for a small consideration, the owners consent to open their doors on rare occasions. Oh, by the way, Lorraine, I forgot to tell you that Edith won't be accompanying us on this jaunt, or to the dinner either. She says she's tired after all that sightseeing this morning, but I'm afraid that nasty mishap with the lift doors has left her rather more shaken than she will admit.'

'And where do you have dinner?' I asked.

'At a hotel in Woodstock, where three well-known mystery writers who live in the area have kindly accepted an invitation to join us.'

'Oh, I see. Well, thank you for explaining it to me. They are neither of them places I had associated with crime. It makes you think.'

'It does indeed, and you may take my word for it, Miss Crichton, there's a lot more about than some of us realise.'

11

There was still an hour left before I was due at the theatre and, away from home, the hour between five and six can pass in leaden minutes, so I decided to use up some of them on a courtesy call. There was no need to ask for directions, for I had been there once before and, when I had knocked on the door, she bade me enter, adding that it was unlocked.

The remains of afternoon tea were on the table, proving that Robin and I were not the only guests to have trays brought to their rooms, and she was standing with her back to me, taking down a cream-coloured coat from the wardrobe.

'Yes, you may take the tray, thank you, Maureen,' she said, still without turning round.

'What would you like me to do with it when I have?' I asked.

She froze completely for a second or two, then slowly turned to face me, leaving the coat dangling on its hanger.

'My goodness, what a nice surprise! Please excuse me, my dear, I thought you were the waitress.'

'And I must be excused for barging in. I was on my way to my room and I decided to look in and see how you were and if there was anything you needed.'

'Well, isn't that kind! Now that you are here, do sit down and talk to me for a while.'

'But haven't I chosen a bad moment? I saw Marilou leave on the bus and I took it for granted you'd be on your own.'

'Yes and, as you see, your reasoning was correct.'

'Except that . . . well, were you planning to go out, by any chance?'

'Oh, my gracious, no, whatever can have given you that idea? Ah, I do believe I can guess. It was the coat?'

'Yes, I had the impression you were taking it out of the cupboard, not putting it away.'

'As indeed I was and perhaps I may ask you to finish the task for me? I find the evenings here a little chilly for these old bones and Marilou went flying off, forgetting all about putting my shawl out.'

'Then tell me where it is and I'll get it for you. I'm sure you'd be much more comfortable in a shawl.'

'Thank you, my dear. It's the white one on the middle shelf of the closet. The door is inclined to stick and you'll need to give it a good sharp pull.'

As it happened, to anyone without arthritic hands it needed nothing of the kind, but I made a pretence of having to struggle with it, to spare her feelings.

'Oh, and while you're up, dear, would you save me another journey by fetching my ring? I left it in the bathroom and this is one of those good old-fashioned hotels, with a real live chambermaid coming in to turn down the bed, and I wouldn't want to put temptation in anyone's way.'

'There we go,' I said when I had handed her the ring, draped the shawl round her shoulders and rehung the coat.

'And now, after all that labour, why not sit down and tell me some news, if you can spare the time? Oh, listen to me, I nearly forgot! First off, I want to thank you personally for that beautiful posy you sent me. Lavender is my favourite perfume. Shall I order you some tea, or is it time for something stronger?'

'Nothing for me, thank you. I have to be in the theatre in about half an hour.'

'And I can tell, just from our brief acquaintance, that you're strict about keeping to your routine.'

'Whereas something I've learned about you, Mrs Dearing, is that you're strong on intuition. And I do hope you'll be able to come to the play tomorrow. I've earmarked the aisle seat in the third row, which is the nearest to the exit, and there's also a ramp beside the stairs down to the stalls. Everything's fixed with the Front of the House Manager.'

'But how thorough! What did you need to fix with him?'

'Arrangements for your wheelchair. He's agreed that during the performance it can either be folded up and left in the cloakroom, or just stacked by the entrance to the stalls, whichever suits you best.'

'Well, I do appreciate your going to all this trouble. My goodness, you people are kind! But I assure you it won't be necessary to bring the darn contraption inside. It can quite well be left on the bus and I'll hobble the rest of the way. I can manage that with no trouble at all. Only reason I need the chair is not to have to slow the others down to my snail's pace.'

'Well, if you're sure?'

'Quite sure. Now I know there are no stairs to bother about, I shall feel quite secure. Stairs can be a worry and that's why I decided to stay home tonight. Apparently, the ghost only walks in one of the attic bedrooms, so that would have been a waste of time from my point of view.'

'Although it seems a shame that you had to miss the dinner too. Couldn't you have whiled away the time downstairs while they were bedroom prowling? Or did you perhaps make a deliberate choice there, as well?'

'Now, what would give you that idea, I wonder?'

'Well, they had invited three authors to meet you, I understand?'

'And you think that might have been too much excitement for me?'

'Not in the least, but it did occur to me that, being writers, presumably at least one of them might have recognised you and might also have remembered that Edith Mae McClintock had married someone called Dearing. Conceivably, that might also have been why you sent Marilou to the bookshop on her own this afternoon? Some of those assistants have long memories.'

She gave me a thoughtful look and said: 'You can be very vexing sometimes, Tessa, for all your kind heart and pretty manners. This is not the first time you have accused me of being a writer in disguise.'

'I know. I can't tell you why, but there was something about you which gave me the idea the minute I met you. Are you going to tell me I was quite wrong?'

'Oh, it's true enough, otherwise I wouldn't be vexed. I might even feel flattered, for all I know. What bothers me is who else you might have told.'

'Not a soul, I promise you, but would it have been so tragic and terrible if I had?'

'It certainly would. It would upset my plans and few things can be more tragic than that when you get to my age and have so little left to plan for.'

'I'm sorry, Mrs Dearing. That's the last thing I'd want to do to anyone, least of all you, whose books always gave me such huge enjoyment.'

'You certainly know how to get round a person, don't you, Tessa? You are now forgiven?'

'Thank you. And so will you indulge me still further by explaining how it is that your being a celebrated author . . .'

'Correction. Used to be.'

'Used to be a celebrated author could interfere with your plans?'

'The answer is that I am hoping to make some kind of comeback.'

'Oh, that's terrific news, although it does deepen the mystery still further.'

'Ah, but you see I mean to branch out and create a whole new style and identity. No more of these dated little heroines in colonial mansions, whose hearts miss a beat every time a certain gentleman walks into the room. It may be too late, but I want to move on. I can't manage pens or typewriters any more, I have to rely on Marilou for that, as for so much else, but I still have part of my brain left and I intend to use it, if I can.'

'When did this idea hit you?'

98

'I've been thinking about it off and on for several years, ever since my husband died, but somehow other things got in the way.'

'Is that why you came on this trip? To put yourself in the mood, as it were?'

'The girl's a marvel! How did you guess?'

'Not very clever, really. I thought it might have something to do with the urge to soak up some atmosphere.'

'Ah well, in a sense, yes, but there was more to it than that. The truth is that a month or two back someone, and I don't even recollect any more who it was, told me a strange and rather alarming story concerning one of these travel agencies who make big business out of specialty tours. It was just the kind of starting-point I'd been searching around for. They're springing up all over the country just now, so no problem with libel. Furthermore, the Bridge of San Louis Rey situation, with a dozen or so strangers thrown together by chance and cut off from the outside world, is a classic theme and this would provide a new variation. Then, just a few days afterwards, I was in my doctor's waiting room, looking through a back number of the *New Yorker*, and there it was, staring me in the face.'

'What was?'

'A discreet little announcement from the High and Wide Travel Bureau with their schedule of specialised trips to Europe, beginning with a Mystery Readers' Tour of Britain at the end of May. Well, I have my superstitions, like most people do, I guess, and that sounded like a message not to be ignored. So here I am, a wolf in sheep's clothing among the innocent herd, pretending to be a true, blue, wide-eyed believer. Isn't that a shameful confession?'

'No, on the contrary, I consider it very strong-minded of you not to have given yourself away. Just imagine how thrilled the sheep would be to discover they were in the company of a real live mystery writer, and how they'd be able to boast about it when they got home. On the other hand, I suppose I can also see how it might have made them feel uncomfortable and self-conscious. They would never quite have managed to shake off the feeling that you were watching them and listening to every word, with the intention of putting them in a book. It would have spoilt everything.'

'You're right there, too. I'm afraid it's a misconception which so many people do have about writers.'

'Except that, in this case, it would have been true, wouldn't it? Be honest, Mrs Dearing. Isn't that exactly what you are up to?'

'But of course,' she admitted cheerfully. 'Since you have seen through me like a pane of glass, why should I trouble to deny it? And now I know you have to run along, so I mustn't keep you here chatting, much as I'm enjoying your company. It was so kind of you to drop by.'

'Yes, I ought to leave in a minute,' I agreed, feeling slightly relieved to know that she would have had some difficulty in pushing me out by force, 'but before I do, won't you tell me how it's coming along?'

'Pretty well, I'd say. As you see, there are numerous restrictions on my movements, but I've learned to live with them now and I'm having a good time, by and large.'

'I'm delighted to hear it, but I was really referring to work on the book. Apart from providing such a promising situation, you must have found plenty of copy among your fellow travellers, haven't you?'

'Oh, some of them have come up with bits and pieces here and there, but they'll get all mixed up with bits and pieces from other people and their own mothers wouldn't recognise them the way they'll end up. And I doubt if I'll be drawing on the more flamboyant among them, with quirks and characteristics which stand out a mile. One can accept the existence of people like that in real life, but they would seem exaggerated in fiction.'

'I'm sure you're right, but all the same I do hope you mean to take a few bits and pieces from the Neilsens? They strike me as being an absolute gift to a writer.'

'Why them, in particular?'

'Because they're such an odd, ill-matched pair. I'd have thought they would provide endless opportunities.'

'And how would you handle it, if you were a writer?'

Having already given some thought to the subject, I was able to reply without hesitation:

'Well, first of all, they wouldn't really be married at all. In my story they don't even know each other very well. I realise this means they would have to have separate rooms, but I imagine a pro like you could easily come up with a plausible reason for that?'

'Life has already provided one. They do have separate rooms and the plausible, and no doubt perfectly true, reason is that Cornelius talks in his sleep.'

'Then I think you'll have to improve on life. Speaking as a reader, I don't find it at all plausible. I should wonder how a man who talked so much when he was awake would have any voice left by the time he went to bed.'

'Yes, you make an interesting point there, but my informant was Marilou, who is not given to flights of fancy. And had you arrived at any motive for this charade? An illicit affair, perhaps, with one or other of them on the run from a jealous spouse?'

'Well, no, that would hardly require single bedrooms, would it? And, anyway, I'd prefer something more sinister.'

'Then let me offer a suggestion as my parting gift. I don't intend to use it, so it is no sacrifice. How about if she were a professional psychiatrist and he her patient? He has been bundled out of the country by his family in order to avoid an unpleasant scandal involving, let us say, a young and innocent girl. In the circumstances, it would be too risky to leave him free to roam around on his own in some foreign country, so they have hired this reliable and experienced woman who, for

101

appearances' sake, is masquerading as his wife. Needless to say, they are travelling under her name, not his. How's that for a perfect set-up for blackmail?'

'Brilliant!' I said, blowing her a kiss as I moved to the door. 'Absolutely first-rate. I rather wish you would use it yourself.'

'Oh dear me, no. We couldn't have art imitating life, could we now? That's not allowed in the kind of fiction I write.'

Later that evening Peter Ruskin, an old friend and fellow member of the cast, accompanied me back to the hotel after the performance. He had been trying to get in touch with a television producer, whose private number happened to be in my address book. As there was still half an hour left before closing time, I told him to set us both up with a drink while I went to my room to find it.

When I rejoined him he was sitting at the bar, about a yard away from another man, who was also on his own. So I manoeuvred myself into the gap between them, handed one a slip of paper with the telephone number on it and, turning to the other, wished him good evening.

'How did it go?' I asked. 'Did anyone see the ghost?'

'No, not one of them, which may have been just as well.'

'I shouldn't wonder. Have you met Peter Ruskin? This is Colin Gascoine, Pete, and he's bringing a party to see us tomorrow night.'

'Ah, my dear fellow, how perfectly ripping of you!'

'We're all looking forward to it. Which reminds me, how did things go for you tonight? Good house?'

'Not half bad. Almost full, weren't we, Pete?'

'Capacity. Standing room only, so I am reliably informed.'

He had a ponderous and emphatic way of uttering even the most commonplace remark, both on and off stage, which had effectively typecast him for headmaster and army officer roles and, since these two professions represented a life-style so far removed from his own somewhat raffish one, I always imagined him to be particularly happy and fulfilled man. He was also inclined to be absent-minded and I said:

'You've put Jake's number in a safe place, I trust? Don't get all the way home and find you've lost it.'

'Safe as the Bank of Switzerland,' he replied, patting a pocket at random. 'I intend to make use of it before he leaves the house tomorrow morning.'

'You'll need to be up sharpish, in that case. He has a two-hour drive to work and he leaves at dawn.'

'Oh my God, really? Then it might be more practical to sit up through the watches of the night. However, I shall bid you goodnight now and plod my weary way. Goodnight, sir. I hope you enjoy our little offering and laugh very heartily in all the right places. Goodnight, my darling Tess, see you tomorrow.'

Colin's glass was also now empty and I said:

'How about you? You must be feeling pretty whacked too, after all you've been through.'

'Far from it, just beginning to wake up. This is my favourite hour of the day and better than ever this evening, if I may make so bold. In fact, I intend to spin it out by ordering another drink. Can I persuade you to join me?'

'No, thanks, I'll make do with this. I don't mind spinning for another ten minutes, however. I'm another who likes to unwind slowly. Could we move to a table, though? I simply hate being perched up here, with my legs dangling and nowhere to put my bag.'

'I have a question for you,' he said, when this matter had been attended to, 'if you don't mind?'

'I don't mind at all because I have one for you. Let's start with yours.'

'Why were you taken aback to find I was English?'

'Well, it was stupid, I suppose, but I knew this tour had been masterminded by an American firm and I just somehow took it for granted. Still, lots of British people seem to have jobs over there nowadays and vice versa.'

'I daresay they do, but I'm not one of them. I've only been to the States once in my life and that was on my honeymoon. My

103

employers are called Eros Tours and they're based in Gloucester. You could hardly get more English than that.'

'No, I'd got it completely wrong. Either that, or Lorraine did.
I thought she told me everything had been arranged through a
firm in Baltimore.'

'She was quite right, but the way things work is that they set
the project up and sell it to the customers. It's then passed over
to us to work out the detailed itinerary and take charge as they
step out of the plane at Heathrow. Both firms make a very good
thing out of it, but they're separate companies, operating for
the most part quite independently. Your turn now.'

'In view of what you've just told me, mine is no longer worth
asking. Now you've explained the set-up, I realise you'd be in
no better position to answer it than the barman, conceivably
less so.'

'Oh, come, Miss Crichton, don't be too hard on me.'

'Do call me Tessa. Everyone does.'

'And proud to be of their number. Thank you, Tessa. I find it
hard to believe that my single qualification was in either being
American, or at least knowing the country well. You are
surrounded by people who fill both those requirements.'

'No, I had depended on your being particularly well informed
about the travel business over there. To come right to the point,
I was going to ask if there was anything you could tell me about
a woman called Barbara Landauer.'

'Who was murdered about a week ago, not a stone's throw
from where you were staying, so I've heard tell. Not a lot, no.'

'But you do know something? Did you ever meet her, by the
way?'

'No, never. She was a compatriot of ours, of course, but as
far as I know she hadn't lived here for years. I know of her,
however, as do a great many people in our business.'

'And didn't much care for what you did know?'

'I never said so.'

'No, but your voice took on that guarded note which people
often use when they are falling over themselves not to say
anything they might live to regret.'

'I assure you, Tessa, there was no danger of that. It is true that she had a reputation for being ambitious and ruthless in furthering her own ends, often at someone else's expense, but that comes under the heading of hearsay and a lot of it could have been jealousy, for all I know. Besides, there was nothing anyone in my humble position could have known or possessed which could conceivably have been either useful or threatening, so I'd have been quite safe from her attentions.'

'Ruthless and ambitious about money?'

'In all ways, I gather. Power, money, fame, all fuel to her flames.'

'How interesting! And I apologise for asking so many questions when you had only bargained for one, but I'll try and make this the last. Did High and Wide Travel Bureau ever have any dealings with her?'

'Yes, at one time I gather they did. That's how I picked up the little I know about her. I don't get invited over to the States, worse luck, but the directors of our stepsister company visit us here from time to time, mainly to check out the hotels on our list and generally keep us up to the mark, but we try to ensure that they have a good time when the day's work is done. It's during those evening sessions that subjects like these tend to get bandied about and one picks up stray bits of information.'

'And it was kind of you to dredge a few of them up for me.'

'Oh, I may be able to improve on that performance, with any luck. Mr Richard Ginsberg, the company president, no less, with be spending a few days here, with his daughter, very shortly. In fact, he means to join us for the last couple of days of the Mystery Tour.'

'Really? Is that a normal routine?'

'By no means, but I imagine he either has other business over here as well, or is combining this with a holiday. Knowing him, though, I am sure he has his reasons and one of them might be an on-the-spot inspection of the New Westminster, since it's the first time we've had it on our list. I suspect he might also see it as a chance for a little PR work. We have one or two fairly influential people in the current bunch and Mr Ginsberg, who is

105

not one to let so much as a blade of grass grow under his feet, might feel it would be a smart move to establish some personal contacts. I'll do a bit of fishing for you and see what I can pull out. Are you sure you won't have another drink?'

'No, thanks awfully, it's past my bedtime already. What an unusual man you've turned out to be.'

'Have I? That's good. I was hoping to make an impression, of course.'

'Oh, you have, and what impresses me most is your singular lack of curiosity. You haven't once asked me why I'm so curious about Barbara Landauer.'

'There was no need to. I'd worked it out all by myself.'

'Honestly? And what was your conclusion?'

'Well, the fact is that I already knew your husband was in the CID. Nothing clever about that, everyone knows it and, if they didn't before, Lorraine will have seen to that. So I put two and two together, the first one being that he was in charge of the case and the second that you were trying to dig out as much background information as you could from sources which would normally be closed to him. How's that?'

'Very good, most perspicacious of you,' I said, having decided instantly that this explanation, improbable as it was in reality, would do very nicely. Far better that he should carry away illusions about the role of a Detective Inspector's wife than suspect for one moment that it was the possible connection between Barbara Landauer's murder and a member of the Mystery Readers' Tour which had prompted my questions.

12

Aware that the following day's mystery schedule included a visit to Worcester, there to be escorted round the cathedral and porcelain factory by a local author and former captain of the country cricket eleven, I had not expected to get a glimpse of the party until the evening. However, when I emerged from the bathroom just after 10.00 a.m. there was a hammer blow on the door and two seconds later Lorraine wafted in, kicked off her shoes and subsided full-length on to the bed, where she remained with eyes closed.

'More trouble?' I enquired after a moment or two.

'In the plural. I no sooner deal with one than another comes creeping up and attacks me from behind.'

'How about starting with the one you were meeting head on?'

'It was Beverly, as usual, although for a while Virginia and I thought we had it sorted out.'

'You refer to Colin's ultimatum, no doubt? Was your policy to try and persuade him to let her stay on, or to do as he asked and take her home?'

'The second. Virginia had every sympathy with his claim that Beverly would inevitably get into more trouble if she stayed, and she also gave out some strong hints that it was up to me to pick up the pieces and take them back to the States.'

'So, having got that worked out, what went wrong?'

'Just about everything. We'd thrashed it out before saying a word to Beverly, you see. It was while they were ghost-hunting and we grabbed the chance to take a stroll in the garden. It was such a hideous, uncomfortable house, I should imagine the ghost had given up visiting centuries ago and found some better place to haunt. Anyway, Bev was very scared, or pretended to be, in case they did see him and she was clinging on to Cornelius on one side and Ed on the other, which gave me the chance to tell Virginia in private about the shoplifting episode.'

'I'd been meaning to ask you about that. Did Beverly refer to it herself?'

'No, not a word. Mind you, there hadn't been much opportunity. She was upstairs with Edith and she didn't come down until two minutes before the bus left.'

'How was she on the drive to Banbury? Nervous, repentant?'

'Neither of those. She was quieter than usual. That was Edith's good influence, I guess. She's so down-to-earth herself and she won't stand for any play-acting, so Bev doesn't try it on with her. It didn't take her long to work through it, though.'

'And then back to the histrionics?'

'I couldn't be sure it was that, or whether she genuinely believed what she was telling us. How could anyone know?'

'What did she tell you?'

'When we came back here after dinner, at around ten o'clock, Virginia and I went up to her room with her and broke the news that we'd been told about the shoplifting.'

'What was her reaction?'

'Not so bad at the start. She was mutinous, but calm about it and not one bit ashamed. Just kept repeating over and over that she hadn't stolen anything, that it was all a frame-up and someone had planted the stuff on her.'

'Had she any theories about who it might have been, or for what purpose?'

'Did she ever? First off, she said it had to be one of the shop assistants, who was anti-American, of all damn silly ideas. When she saw she couldn't get away with that, she said maybe, on second thoughts, it was some professional thief who had used her as a temporary dumping ground with the intention of getting the stuff back when she moved to another department.

Well, I don't know, but I guess there could be something in that, couldn't there? What do you think?'

'Not a lot. How was Virginia taking it?'

'Like you, not seriously. So then we came down to the business, how she and I would be taking a plane home tomorrow and leaving the other two to finish out the vacation on their own.'

'Which didn't go down very well?'

'She went to pieces, screaming and wailing and pulling her hair out. I was terrified one of the other guests would hear and complain to the management, but luckily these walls seem to be as thick as the people who run the place.'

'What was the gist of her complaint? Simply that she was enjoying herself and didn't feel like going home just yet?'

'No, she never claimed to be enjoying it, just that she refused to leave and if anyone wanted to try and make her, they'd have to knock her unconscious and carry her on to the plane. Frankly, Tessa, I was tempted to take her at her word.'

'What's so terrible about going home, I wonder? An admission of defeat, perhaps? Having to acknowledge that she wasn't completely cured, after all?'

'I honestly don't know. She kept howling that it was a plot and we were trying to trick her.'

'In what way?'

'Into going back into that clinic. Not Bella Vista, but that ghastly place she was in before. I tried to get it through to her that such an idea had never entered anyone's head. I said if she didn't choose to go home, or have anyone know she'd cut the tour short, there'd be no problem. She and I would go down to Florida or to the West Coast for a few days and then we'd all meet up again in New York. It didn't do any good. She just went on screaming that it was a trick. We'd get on some plane and I'd pretend it was bound for Florida and, sure enough, we'd end up at this place in Arizona, or wherever, and they'd be waiting for her. She'd be taken away and locked up in a cell.'

109

'Did she really believe that, do you suppose?'

'Who knows, but it sounded genuine to me. Virginia doesn't agree, but then I wouldn't expect her to. She just wants Beverly out of her hair and the sooner the better. Bringing her was Ed's idea in the first place and I bet she's been regretting she ever agreed to it.'

'But she must have realised when they took it on how easily it could go wrong?'

'I doubt if she has that much imagination and no one could have forseen just how wrong it would go. Beverly has been a different girl ever since she crossed the Atlantic. Things started to get out of hand the very first day.'

'And we both know where she spent her very first day and what happened there, don't we, Lorraine?'

'Well, I realise you believe there's some connection with that woman's murder, but don't forget it was also the day she lost her camera. Maybe that's at the root of it.'

'And now that she's found it again, wouldn't you expect her to be returning to normal?'

'She hasn't found it again, at least not that one. The gold chain on the one she has now is a fake.'

'How do you know?'

'Virginia says so and I believe her. She may lack imagination, but she's shrewd and she does know about the value of things.'

'The more I hear about that girl, Lorraine, the more I consider that Ed made a big mistake in allowing himself to be dragged back to the altar. However, too late to worry about that now. How did Virginia discover the chain was a fake?'

'When she came in this afternoon with all her purchases, and while Beverly was safely tied up with Edith, she went to the desk and asked for her room key.'

'Oh, is that all? What an anticlimax!'

'Not her own key, Beverly's.'

'Oh yes, and then let herself in and searched the place, I suppose?'

'Didn't take long. The bag was there on the bed, the one she uses for carrying lingerie around in, and the camera and chain were inside it. One quick inspection was all it needed.'

'Did she then tackle Beverly about it?'

'No, fortunately she didn't have the chance and I advised her to keep quiet for a while. I said we had enough problems on our hands without taking on more. There's still Colin's ultimatum hanging over us, which has to be the first priority.'

'So what have you finally decided to do? Beg for mercy and one more chance?'

'I would, if I thought it would do any good, but I don't.'

'Then you would appear to be on the horns?'

'Yeah, I know, that's what I wanted to talk with you about.'

'Well, don't expect much help from me, Lorraine. Short of chloroforming her for the duration, I can't see any way out. Is that what you've done with her now, by the way? Or is she, even as we speak, wandering about and creating more mayhem?'

'No, chloroforming is nearer. Virginia finally managed to get her to take a sleeping pill at around midnight, but before that she'd had the bright idea of switching rooms. Ed spent the night in Beverly's room and Beverly has moved in with Virginia.'

'How about your trip to Worcester this morning?'

'Ed and Virginia will go on their own and I'll stay here and take care of Beverly. Virginia can't wait to get her hands on some of that reject china. She sees herself walking off with an entire porcelain dinner service for around fifty dollars. Bev was still asleep when they left. Furthermore, the door's locked and I have the key. So, provided she doesn't smash it down, or set fire to the place, we can relax for a while.'

'All the same, you can't keep these emergency measures going indefinitely. If Colin won't relent and Beverly refuses to go home, where does that leave you?'

'Well, I do have a plan ... but ... the thing is, to some extent, it involves your co-operation.'

'Oh, dear!'

'Nothing terrible, I swear.'

'Go on, spit it out!'

'All I need right now is for you to fix with the box-office for two of our seats for tonight to be exchanged for two in another part of the house. Got it?'

'You mean yours and Beverly's, of course, but is that wise? It's a very small theatre, I should remind you.'

'It's the best I can do. It would really break her up if she had to miss the show tonight and that could only lead to worse trouble. I take full responsibility. As soon as they get in from Worcester, I'll tell Colin that I've called the travel people in Baltimore to let them know we're leaving the tour for personal reasons, no reflection on him, and we're now born-again private citizens. Then tomorrow Basil can drive us into London and we'll spend the rest of the time there, having a ball in the shops and theatres. We'll travel back the same day, but by different airlines. Beverly will be quite set up by then, if I have anything to do with it, and we'll take trunks full of gifts for Lynn. She'll never have to know that anything went wrong.'

'Unless, for example, it should occur to Virginia to mention the little matter of a gold chain which disappeared and turned up again as a fake?'

'I thought of that, too, and I mean to fix her, if she tries a trick like that. I told you our itinerary would include an attack on the London shops. Well, one of my favourite haunts is a jeweller in the Burlington Arcade. They can work miracles there and ever since Henry spent a couple of hours with them last time he was over, they've been able to work them even faster.'

'So Fairy Twinkletoes has thought of everything. Congratulations, and I hope you bring it off. Where will you be staying in London?'

'Back at the little old New Westminster. It's pretty crummy, but it will do for a start, anyway. Well, back to my charge now and see how she reacts to the idea of driving up to Stratford and having lunch by the river. Basil's all set to move off when we give the word.'

(2)

I took the precaution of arriving a quarter of an hour before my usual time at the theatre, in the hope of finding a number of

112

applicants already lined up at the box-office for tickets for the evening performance. This turned out to have been a slightly over-optimistic calculation, but there were three or four people ahead of me in the queue and, after an interval of several minutes, two more had fallen in behind, of which the second was Mervyn Houghton.

I had banked on his not putting himself to the risk of any financial outlay in order to disprove my assertion that the theatre was sold out for every performance, so was unprepared for this and presented him with my back view only, staring straight ahead and trying to pretend I was someone else.

It did not work, however. Edging the man in front of him to one side, he moved close enough to give me a sharp tap on the shoulder, while booming out for all to hear:

'Hello, what's this then? Don't tell me it's part of your job to stand out here for ten minutes every evening, making out you're a customer?'

'No, just arranging about the house seats for some friends of mine. And you? Are you a customer, or just looking?'

'Oh, deadly serious. My mama, whose word is law, had to come in to parley with her accountant this afternoon and hit on the notion of coming here afterwards. I've been sent ahead to collect the tickets and make sure all is in order.'

'Well, I hope she enjoys it. Where are you sitting?'

'Stalls somewhere. Can't remember which row. Thirteen or fourteen, anyhow, so we should be pretty well in the centre.'

'Not on the aisle, I'm afraid,' I remarked, feeling pleased about this since it was no part of my newly formed plan to sacrifice Edith Dearing's comfort on the altar of my scheming.

'Never mind. Best I could do at short notice. Matter of fact, in view of what you told me, I was a bit surprised to find they had anything left at all. Only rang 'em up at lunchtime.'

'Ah well,' I explained, 'in a case like this, it's always best to leave it till the last minute. More chance of a few returns having come in.'

It was now my turn at the box-office and, moving into position, I added:

113

'Want me to collect yours for you, while I'm at it?'

'Not a bad idea. Hang on for the space of one second and I'll give you the piece of plastic.'

Having done so, he then, as I had hoped, promptly left his place in the queue, which had no doubt been a somewhat irksome one for a man of his station in life, thereby allowing me to conduct my business in private.

It took a minute or two to complete, involving, as it did, some complicated hanky-panky and a certain amount of switching around of tickets and envelopes. As a result, the Houghtons came off very well. The two seats originally allotted to them were right at the back of the stalls, whereas those they actually received were in the third row and were officially priced at an extra two pounds each. From my point of view, though, they carried the advantage that Mervyn would be in close range of Colin Gascoine for over two hours at a stretch. He was not one to whom self-effacement came naturally and I had hopes that such prolonged and close proximity might evoke, if not recognition, some stirrings of memory in Colin, which linked up with other memories concerning Barbara Landauer.

13

A quick look through the curtain peephole before the house lights went down revealed that the cast in front appeared to have taken up their positions according to plan. I could not be certain that the red hair in the back row belonged to Beverly, but it was a fair guess that it did and, more to the point, every seat in the third row was occupied.

I had an even better opportunity to satisfy myself on this point in the scene where I had to apply the soothing touch to Boss Mangan's poor squeezed head, the director having thoughtfully positioned me centre stage behind the seated Mangan and directly facing the audience. However, on this occasion it was I who almost fell into a trance when, for a perilous moment which could so easily have proved fatal, I found my concentration sliding away as I stared out at the upturned faces and saw to my astonishment that the seat in which I had last seen Colin was now occupied by Lorraine.

I recovered myself in the nick of time and, by resolutely shutting out all extraneous thoughts, managed to get through the rest of the scene without losing my lines or collapsing into nervous giggles.

The discipline was so successful that by the interval I had forgotten all about the near lapse and the memory only returned when, back in my room after the final curtain, I received two unexpected callers in the persons of Mervyn and his mother. Any sense of gratification I might have felt for this attention, however, quickly evaporated as it became clear that the purpose of their visit was not to congratulate me on my performance.

Having waited for them to begin and discovered that they were not going to, I asked how they had enjoyed the play and Mervyn replied that it was a bit like the curate's egg, if I knew what he meant, and then proceeded to explain what he meant.

His mother, on the other hand, took a more constructive line. She told me that she had seen *Heartbreak House* when she was a girl and it had quite stuck in her mind. To this day she could describe the dress she had worn for the occasion and furthermore that very celebrated actress, whose name had slipped her mind for the moment, had taken the part of Mrs Hushabye and I could call her old-fashioned, if I liked, but she maintained that none of this lot nowadays could hold a candle to her.

'You need to speak up a bit more,' she announced, turning the attack directly on me. 'All that muttering and whispering won't do at all. I could pick up most of it because I happen to have very sharp hearing, but goodness knows what the rest of the audience made of it.'

'I always see Ellie as a very quiet sort of girl,' I replied, stung, as she had meant me to be, by this criticism. 'She manages to make her point in a subtle way, without a lot of shouting and hectoring.'

'Shouting doesn't come into it,' Mrs Houghton informed me. 'It is a question of voice projection. No good trying to be subtle if they can't hear a word in the upper circle.'

It hardly seemed worth while pointing out that the theatre did not have an upper circle and, instead, I apologised for my inability to offer them a drink, then waited for them either to go away or to account for their presence. The most likely one, in my opinion, was that Mrs Houghton needed to round off every evening with a bit of bullying, which had the effect on her of a hot toddy, and that I happened to be the nearest fodder for the purpose.

However, at this point Mervyn came up with the true explanation which equally unsurprisingly, proved to be a pecuniary one:

'Met a friend of yours out there,' he said. 'Sitting next to me.'

'Oh, really? Who was that?'

116

'American. Woman called Lorraine Thurloe.'

'Fancy that! And how did you know she was a friend of mine?'

'Told me so. Went on about it all through the interval.'

'My goodness, how boring for you!'

'I didn't mind. Charming creature, I thought. Bit naïve, perhaps, but none the worse for that. Mama took to her, too, and we're all for this hands-across-the-sea lark.'

'Yes, of course you are, it plays a big part in your affairs now, doesn't it? And Lorraine told you her name?'

'It came out. She was telling me she lived in New York, so naturally I asked her whereabouts in New York and what she did and so forth. Only civil.'

'To which she replied that she didn't do much of anything, but was married to a lawyer who was dotty about art and culture and she spent most of her time plodding round museums and galleries with him.'

'Practically verbatim.'

'One of the very best type of Americans,' Mrs Houghton remarked, entering the fray. 'How did you come to meet her?'

'Ah well, she wasn't always married to a lawyer who was dotty about art and culture, you know. We met in more raffish days. I daresay it filtered through to you, Mervyn, that he's pretty well off, as well as cultivated?'

'Don't know about that, but the extraordinary part is that I may have met him.'

'Really? In London?'

'No, New York, when I was over there fixing up a few loose ends three or four months ago. Chap I know invited me to lunch at his club and introduced us. I'm pretty sure this other fellow's name was Thurloe, so they're probably the same man.'

'Well, I never! What an interesting time you've had! No wonder the play seemed rather tame in comparison. I hope you won't think me rude if I throw you out now, but I'm supposed to join some friends for supper at eleven and I'm going to be very, very late if I don't look out.'

In order to underline the point, I turned my head sideways

and went to work on the cold cream and tissues. Evidently, though, Mervyn had overlooked the fact that it was a triple mirror and, reflected in its left panel, I saw him furtively and in one continuous movement stretch out an arm, leaning sideways towards his mother as he did so, then withdraw it again and resume an upright posture.

'Yes, yes, we must go too, past Mama's bedtime,' he said, hauling himself upright now, so that all I could see of him was his stomach. 'She's taken quite a shine to your friend, Lorraine, by the way, haven't you, Mama? We wondered how you'd take to the idea of bringing her up for a dish of tea, or a glass of sherry wine, on Sunday? Gather you'll be at Roakes for the weekend, too?'

'On Sunday?' I repeated. 'Whatever gave you that idea? She'll be going back to America in a few days and, as far as I know, she has no plans to go to Roakes for the weekend.'

'Not the way it sounded to me. May be wrong, of course, but might be worth checking.'

'Yes, it might. Goodnight, Mrs Houghton, and thank you so much for coming round. It was most kind of you.'

They both went out and two-and-a-half minutes later came the expected rap on the door. Evidently taking silence as permission to enter, Mervyn did so.

'Sorry to be a bore, but Mama thinks she left her specs behind.'

'Yes, she did. You'll find them on that chair in front of you. They'd fallen on the floor, so it's lucky you didn't step on them as you went out.'

'All part of the charmed life she leads. Matter of fact, there's something I want to ask you, now I'm here.'

'OK, but don't forget I'm in a raging hurry, will you?'

'Won't take a second. It's about that chap who had the seat next to mine in the theatre. You wouldn't happen to know who he was?'

'No. How would I? And, anyway, five minutes ago you were telling me that Lorraine had the seat next to yours.'

'That was later. When we arrived there was a man sitting

there. After a couple of ticks he got up and moved off. Then later, when we were making for the exit, I saw him again with a red-haired girl in tow.'

'So, obviously, he was someone who'd realised he was in the wrong seat. It's not important, surely?'

'Probably not. You're certain you don't know who he could have been?'

'I can't see any reason why I should and, at the risk of sounding rude, I really am late for an appointment.'

'No, I hadn't forgotten. Just wanted to make sure. Some funny blokes about nowadays. Can't be too careful.'

'Is that meant to be a warning of some kind?'

'Warning? No, course not, but I've seen that chap somewhere before, take my oath on it and there's something odd about him. As I say, can't be too careful.'

When he had gone, I wasted another five minutes at the table, pulling faces at myself as I considered whether this had been the equivalent of the nub of a four-page letter being contained in the one-line postscript and whether the correct word in my question would have been, not warn, but threaten.

(2)

'Very late indeed,' I agreed, 'for which I apologise, but if you'd be interested to hear who's to blame for it, the answer is that you are. What do you mean by changing seats in midstream and upsetting all my carefully laid plans?'

'Not my doing. Blame it on Colin.'

'How did it come about?'

'He came back to where Bev and I were sitting and beckoned me out to the aisle. I thought he was going to say Edith had had a heart attack, or something, but it wasn't that at all. He'd been looking round to see what kind of audience it was and he'd noticed us in the back row. That worried him so much he got to feeling guilty about it and he wanted to switch places with me. I told him there was no need and I had a neck like a giraffe, so it didn't bother me where I sat, but he wouldn't listen and I finally gave in and did as I was told.'

'I'm sure he's got a crush on you. He must have realised it

would mean his sitting with Beverly. Wasn't that rather disagreeable for him?'

'He said he could handle it and keep her in order, if necessary. His attitude was that, now he's no longer officially responsible, he can get tough with her any time he needs to. It must have worked too. She was very docile when I picked her up in the foyer afterwards, and she went upstairs like a lamb the minute Virginia said the word. Anyway, I don't see what all this has to do with your being half an hour late.'

'Well, unfortunately, that chivalrous gesture had far wider repercussions than Colin could have forseen. Which reminds me, Lorraine, you didn't say anything to me about going to Roakes next Sunday.'

'I was going to, but the idea only came into my head some time this evening.'

'Really? Who put it there, I wonder?'

'What's the matter with you? Don't you like him, or something? He told me he was an old friend and neighbour of Toby's and that he'd had lunch with you only a week or two ago. You'll have to brief me in advance if there are a lot of old friends and neighbours of Toby's running around who I'm not supposed to speak to.'

'It wasn't your fault. Those pearls you're wearing tonight were enough to seal your fate. Besides, Mervyn is like a lot of arrogant people. He's so conscious of the honour he confers on others by making himself agreeable that they take him at his own valuation and feel suitably grateful.'

'OK, so I'm simple-minded and I fell for it, but where's the harm? We don't have to follow it up and I don't have to go to Roakes on Sunday.'

'You know damn well that wasn't the cause of my complaint. Of course you do. Toby will be thrilled to bits and you and I will go and call on the Houghtons for half an hour. You live such a sheltered life that it will be a real eye-opener for you to see a thoroughly beastly family in full cry.'

'And Beverly too, don't forget.'

'Oh yes, Beverly. What a nuisance! Never mind, that might be interesting, in its way. At the very least, she'll say something outrageous enough to render the old harridan speechless for a couple of minutes, which would make it all worth while.'

'And at best?'

'Well, you never know, do you? It may not be beyond the bounds of possibility that the sight of Mervyn will stir up some latent memory. Oh, of course, you don't know about that, do you? I'll explain some time, but it's all mixed up with Barbara Landauer and the ghost, who might or might not have been walking on Roakes Common that famous afternoon.'

14

The rest of the night passed uneventfully, so far as I was concerned, but others were less fortunate, notably Ed, who was awakened at three in the morning by an unknown intruder.

He was aroused from a healthy sleep by a light shining directly on to his face. It had vanished by the time he was fully awake and he concluded that it had been the light from a full moon which moments later had been blacked out by a passing cloud. However, as his mind gradually cleared, he recollected that only the night before he had been coerced by Virginia into a boring ritual of bowing three times and churning the loose change around in his pocket, in obeisance to the new moon.

The next conclusion was that there had never been a light at all and he had dreamt it, but this theory also had to be thrown out a moment later by the unmistakable sound of a door opening and closing. By the time he had fumbled with his lightswitch, succeeded in turning it on, climbed out of bed and looked up and down the corridor, there was no one to be seen.

Thoroughly demoralised now and uncertain what was real and what imaginary, the question was settled for him as he made the return journey by the sight of a glove lying on the floor, midway between the door and the bed. It was a man's yellow string glove, very new-looking and identical to one he had been shown at some point during the previous forty-eight hours.

Having satisfied himself on this point, he went back to bed, although not immediately to sleep, a number of nagging worries standing between him and this desirable conclusion to his already disturbed night.

He was not apprehensive about the possibility of the intruder's return and neither had he felt it necessary to alert Virginia, for he considered it safe to assume that Cornelius was by now safely tucked away in his own room, feeling pretty silly, not to mention annoyed with Beverly for having failed to inform him that she was temporarily occupying someone else's bed.

There remained, however, two other causes of perplexity. In his day Ed had, on occasion, paid late-night visits to young ladies in their bedrooms, but, to the best of his recollections, he had never worn gloves for the purpose.

Various explanations came to mind for their presence now, including the far-fetched one that Cornelius, having a childish turn of mind and being heavily under the influence of his current excursion into crime fiction, had seen them as the natural appurtenances of any undercover operation and a safeguard against the wholly imaginary risk of his fingerprints being found on the doorhandle.

In the end, though, he rejected this theory in favour of the slightly more plausible one of the childish turn of mind having manifested itself in a more typical way. In other words, that Cornelius had become so attached to these gloves, which had been bought for a song at the Oxford department store and which he had displayed to one and all as the first essential for the well-turned-out foxhunter, that he could not bear to be parted from them, even transferring them to his dressing-gown pocket when he retired for the night.

However, the most teasing problem of all, which not even Cornelius's immaturity could account for, still remained unsolved. Why would anyone setting forth on an amorous adventure have timed it for three o'clock in the morning?

All this was related to me the following day at second-hand, soon after the touring party had boarded the bus for Cambridge.

Lorraine had hit on the clever notion of arranging for Beverly, to whom no whisper of this incident had been allowed to penetrate, to undergo a heavy programme in a hairdressing salon, with Basil parked outside, ready to gather her up the second she emerged.

'It's the last bit that bothers Ed so much,' Lorraine explained, 'but what worries me is how long this affair has been going on under our noses without our knowing. What's the difference whether it was three o'clock in the morning, or any other time? Only Ed would be dumb enough not to see straight off that Cornelius would have to wait until his wife was out for the count.'

'Not so,' I told her. 'For once, Ed is ahead of you. They sleep in separate rooms. You didn't know?'

'Now how would I know a thing like that?'

'I just thought, with all of you being on the same floor, it might be hard to miss.'

'We aren't always. In some of these smaller places we get spread around, according to what's available. I did know they had a double booking at the New Westminster, but so what? Henry and I often have two rooms when we stay in a hotel, but that doesn't mean that we both don't sleep in the same one. Where did you get your information from, anyway?'

'That fountain of all knowledge, Edith Dearing.'

'Oh well, it's likely to be true in that case, and you see what it means, Tessa?'

'More than I thought, by the sound of it.'

'Don't you remember our very first day, when we came down to Roakes?'

'As though I could forget!'

'Then maybe you also remember what happened that same evening in London? How Cornelius and Beverly tricked me into believing all three of them were going to the movies?'

'Yes, and later, when you ran into Mrs Neilsen in the lift, you got such a curious reaction when you asked how she had enjoyed the film. So now we have the explanation, don't we?'

'I'll say we do. What it means is that she had no idea where

124

her husband was that evening. He could have told her that he still had jet lag, or had eaten something that disagreed with him and was planning on an early night. So off she went to explore the town on her own, believing him to be asleep in his own bed.'

'Too true, I'm afraid. And he and Beverly didn't lose much time, did they? So far as we know, they'd only met twenty-four hours earlier, nearly half of which had been spent in airports or on the plane. It's what they call fast work.'

'Oh, don't joke about it, Tessa, for heaven's sake. If Henry ever gets to hear about it he'll divorce me.'

'I imagine Lynn might be a bit annoyed too, so let's hope neither of them ever does. If I were you, I wouldn't say a word of this to Virginia. That'll close one door, at least, although I have a nasty feeling it may already be too late for precautions of that kind.'

'Why? There's no one else Lynn could hear it from.'

'But hasn't it struck you that this might be a much more serious affair than the kind of shipboard romance you'd taken it for, and likely to end quite differently from the way most of them do? Also that it was solely for that reason that Beverly made such an almighty fuss when it was first mooted that you and she should drop out of the tour?'

'It couldn't have got to that pitch in just barely two weeks.'

'Yes, it could, with someone in her situation. There's a line in the play which puts it in a nutshell. Mrs Hushabye tells Ellie that all girls of her age fall in love with impossible people, especially older people. But there's more to it than that, of course.'

'I wish there weren't because you've said too much already.'

'And, in fact, you don't really need to have it spelt out for you, do you? There are a number of factors which make this situation particularly dodgy, starting with the undeniable one that Cornelius has a weakness for young girls. Not an awful lot of men would find Beverly so devastatingly attractive as to be worth leaving home for, but she has all it takes for Cornelius to do so. Not only young in years, but younger still in experience. A sort of fully developed child, you might say, and not likely to mature very rapidly, in my opinion, if she has a doting father figure to cherish his baby girl.'

Lorraine by this time was scowling at me with such venom that, had I not known her better, I should have felt quite afraid.

'You're really surpassing yourself this morning,' she said. 'Any more to add to the list before I step outside and kill myself?'

'Well, yes, quite a few, as it happens, but I'll gloss over the more trivial of them. Like the fact that he can probably be very endearing when he sets out to charm someone and, if he's to be believed, he certainly has plenty on offer in the material sense. That wouldn't be a negligible attraction for a girl who'd been brought up in luxury and suddenly found herself penniless.'

'I'm disappointed to find that comes under the trivial heading. What else?'

'Oh, his wife, of course. She ought to be our most valuable ally, but no, quite the reverse. She may not actively encourage his infidelities, but she certainly doesn't put many obstacles in his way. To all appearances, she would be just as happy if he did run off with someone else.'

'I wouldn't be too sure of that, Tessa. She may not interfere, but she's watchful and she doesn't miss much, in my opinion.'

'Not enough, perhaps. It would never surprise me if she were taking notes in order to hand them over to her divorce lawyer as soon as she gets home.'

'So what ought I to do?'

'Well, you've made a good start by breaking it up for a few days, and, if I were you, I'd continue on the same lines. I wouldn't fly home on the same day as the others and risk the lovebirds having a romantic reunion in the customs shed. It might even be a good idea to prolong your stay, if you can bear to be parted from Henry for a few more days.'

'It won't be easy, but Beverly has to be the first priority. How

126

am I going to talk her round to the idea, though, and find ways to occupy her, if I succeed?'

'Oh, you'll manage, never fear. You've never been short of imagination. Besides, she's very volatile, isn't she? They both are, come to that, so you have time on your side. Today's tragedy could easily be tomorrow's sad, sweet memory, so it's simply a question of hanging on till tomorrow comes.'

'There's just one thing, though, Tessa. ... Well, did it ever strike you that this might be none of our business?'

'You could say it's none of mine, but you have certainly created the impression that you consider it to be yours.'

'Now, don't go climbing on your high horse. All I meant was that all those stupid things like shoplifting and lying about her camera are one thing, but falling in love with someone and maybe wanting to marry him is something else. Does anyone have a right to interfere in that?'

'Probably not, but the point is that they don't have the power to, either. If this is true love and they're both determined to go on seeing each other, there's nothing in the world that you or anyone else can do about it. Your job is simply to save Beverly from making another stupid mistake, which could only lead to more unhappiness.'

'I guess you're right. So we see you at Roakes on Sunday, OK?'

'Have you spoken to Toby, or rather Mrs Parkes, about it yet?'

'Certainly, I have and it's all fixed. I told her about Basil too and she said he could eat lunch in the kitchen, as the pub gets very crowded on Sundays.'

'And also she'll enjoy having a Rolls parked outside the house for the whole afternoon. And now I suppose I had better get dressed. I have a very powerful gentleman coming down from the London press to take me out to lunch and I need to look my best. Oh, by the way, Lorraine, what did Ed do with that yellow string glove? Do you happen to know?'

'No, I never thought of asking. Why would I? It's not important, is it?'

'I'm not sure, but if you think it over you may agree that it could be very important indeed.'

15

On Saturday night Robin drove me over to Roakes, having sat through the last performance of *Heartbreak House* which, he admitted, had been a marginal improvement on the dress rehearsal.

'Which sounds like damning with faint damns,' I remarked. 'Is that really the best you can do?'

'Oh, listen, you don't need fulsome flattery from me. I should have thought the reviews alone would have enabled even your ego to take a few weeks' rest. Not to mention a half-page interview in the paper this morning.'

'Oh, you read that, did you?'

'With mounting horror. Did you really come out with those pretentious remarks about being at the crossroads of your career and all that bunkum?'

'No, of course not. As far as I remember, we were mainly discussing the terrible problems he's having with his eldest son, who wants to leave school and form a pop group in New Zealand, or somewhere. But he's an old friend and I knew I could rely on him to hit the currently acceptable note. All I had to do was fill in a few details about titles and dates and so on. Speaking of which . . .'

'Which which?'

'Details. Any more on the subject of Barbara Landauer's murder?'

'Nothing of any weight. They hauled Jimmie Peacock in again, but had to set him free a few hours later.'

'That sounds rather frivolous. What was he suspected of?'

'Nothing specific. He's been throwing money around in rather a lavish fashion, standing drinks all round at the pub and so on. They were trying to find out where he'd got it.'

'But no luck, evidently?'

'The story was that his mother had given it to him. She'd been putting a bit by every week out of her pension, until she'd saved enough to have her front room redecorated. When Jimmie found out, he told her she'd be in her grave long before she'd collected enough for that. She'd do better to hand over whatever she'd saved so far to him and he'd do the job for less than half what the local builder would charge. So, all smiles, she'd given him money to buy the materials, plus fifty quid for his time.'

'Well, that should be easy enough to check on.'

'You think so? I doubt if Mrs Peacock ever spoke a word of truth in her life. Naturally, she bore him out in every detail and there were a few dustsheets and paint pots lying about, to lend a touch of verisimilitude.'

'But they weren't convinced?'

'Well, would you be? She's not exactly houseproud, about as feckless as her son, and the last woman in the world to spend money on prettying up her surroundings. Besides, if there had been any money tucked away in the teapot, Jimmie would have found it and blued the lot months ago.'

'So the theory, presumably, is that he's been indulging in a little light blackmail?'

'And a fat chance, in my opinion, of finding out who the victim was, or what dark secret Jimmie knows about him. However, there is one tiny ray of hope.'

'What's that?'

'The constable who called on them formed the opinion that Mrs Peacock was not quite at ease. She is apt to adopt a very ingratiating manner when confronted by someone in uniform, but he was ready for that. He thinks there may have been more to it this time and that she genuinely had got the wind up. So perhaps she knows or at any rate has a damn good idea where this money came from and, if they play it clever, she might be the one to crack.'

'On the other hand, she might not. She may not be nearly so scared of the police finding out where the money came from as she is of incurring the displeasure of someone she regards as infinitely more dangerous and powerful.'

'Oh yes? Like who, for instance?'

'Like a fat man with an orange beard and a formidable mother, for instance.'

'Really, Tessa, you're not seriously pursuing the idea that Mervyn's mixed up in this?'

'Not seriously, no, because I admit it does seem rather far-fetched. On the other hand, he is acting strangely just now. Shall I tell you about him and the old termagant coming round to my room the other night?'

When I had done so, he said:

'Peculiar, I agree, but not exactly incriminating.'

'And I suppose you're also going to say you didn't consider my suggestion of checking up on his movements that afternoon to be worth passing on to Sergeant Matthews?'

'Luckily for me, there was no need to. He'd already done some discreet undercover work on it himself.'

'You don't say! That must have been tricky? Keeping it discreet, I mean?'

'Oh, no names, or anything bald like that. Just a description of the car, registration number and so forth, which he touted round in one or two selected areas. Not to people like Toby, you understand, who've lived here since time began and might have recognised it. He concentrated on the weekenders and retired people who've bought up labourers' cottages and transformed them into gentlemen's residences. A good many of them take a burning interest in local conservation, mainly, one suspects, with a view to safeguarding their own properties, so they keep their eyes skinned; they also tend to converge on the

131

pub by the Common, but they are probably almost unaware of the existence of the real nobs, such as the Houghtons, so it should have been a fertile field.'

'Which proved to be barren?'

'So far. I just wanted you to know that he's not so unimaginative as you might suppose, or so blind to the possibility that someone of ancient lineage, living in a big house, with stacks of money, is necessarily *sans peur* and *sans reproche.*'

'Yes and I'm sorry that it hasn't paid off.'

'Well, don't despair just yet.'

'I don't see much to be hopeful about. If no one was able to come up with anything constructive at the time, they're not likely to do so two or three weeks after the event.'

'Perhaps not, but he's been turning over other stones as well. He prevailed on his Superintendent to let him go to London for a chat with Professor Hollins.'

'Professor . . .? Oh, you mean the butterfly man?'

'That's the one.'

'Well, I'm blowed. It really begins to sound as though he's as suspicious as I am about Mervyn's movements that afternoon. How very unexpected! But surely he didn't ask this Hollins straight out whether he could confirm the alibi of a fellow luncheon guest?'

'Not at all. His excuse for calling was simply to confirm that Sir Mervyn had driven him to the railway station to catch the train to Paddington and, having cleared that up, he was reminded of another small matter he'd like to straighten out, if the Professor would bear with him. The most direct route from Warne Hill to Storhampton did not actually pass through Roakes Common, which had been the scene of the murder that afternoon, but nevertheless lay within a mile or two of it, and he wondered whether by any chance the Professor had happened to notice anyone or anything unusual. Naturally, he went on to explain, he had already put this question to Sir Mervyn, with negative results, but he, after all, had been driving and would necessarily have had his eyes fixed on the road ahead, whereas a passenger, especially one who had trained himself to observe the minutest details of his surroundings, could well have noticed something which, on reflection, might strike him as out of place.'

'None of which got him anywhere, I suppose? Still, it's good news that he's not so over-awed by the Houghton family as I had assumed and one cannot but admire his cheek. I wonder old Hollins didn't throw him out on his ear for wasting a lot of his valuable time with fatuous questions, instead of bending his mind to the drug scene or those maniac drivers on the motorway.'

'Far from it. People are amazingly naïve, you know, in situations of this kind, particularly the clever ones, funnily enough. Hollins thoroughly entered into the spirit of the thing, positively inviting more fatuous questions.'

'Which positively stumped the poor old Sergeant, who had no doubt run out of them by then and was unable to invent any more?'

'No, wait! I might not be able to rival Toby as a professional playwright, but I have learned a thing or two over the years about building up to the climax and this is a good one. Matthews said he realised it was a forlorn hope, since he could well understand that even the most hawk-eyed observer would have been at a disadvantage on this occasion, owing to the speed at which they were doubtless obliged to travel. Hollins replied that, on the contrary, that would have posed no problem. He would have said they were moving at just about the normal speed for winding country roads, in other words averaging something between thirty and thirty-five miles an hour. "Oh, really?" said Matthews. "My understanding was that Sir Mervyn was driving you to the station to catch the fast train and that he was cutting it a bit fine."'

'My goodness, Robin, this is certainly coming along nicely. How did the Professor respond to this?'

'By saying that had been his original understanding too, but

133

he had evidently got it wrong. Houghton had not appeared to be in any particular hurry and, in fact, when they reached Storhampton and the Professor had waved goodbye and made his way to the London platform, it was to discover that he still had nearly half an hour to wait for the next train. Furthermore, it turned out to be a very slow one indeed, stopping at every station to Threwing Junction, where he had to change to another one. There now, what do you make of that?'

'Well, just about everything you could name, but, more to the point, what did the Sergeant make of it? Wasn't he rather bowled over to find his shot in the dark had landed so plumb on target?'

'Indeed, he was. I hardly need tell you that his suggestion had only been intended as an opening gambit, in the gradual process of establishing as nearly as he could what time Mervyn had started on his return journey from the station and whether it would have enabled him to get back to Roakes in time to coincide with the murder. Well, that was a flop in a way because, according to him, although Hollins may not be the archetypal, absent-minded professor, he certainly gave the impression of being somewhat vague about such things as time and distance and, in saying he had spent half an hour cooling his heels on the platform, he could have been exaggerating somewhat. It may not have been half so long, perhaps no more than ten minutes.'

'Didn't anyone see him arrive? Ticket collector, people like that?'

'There isn't one on Sundays, or booking clerk either. If you don't already have a ticket, you pay on the train. However, in Matthew's opinion, there had been something faintly odd about Mervyn's behaviour, as described by Hollins, so he plugged away at that for a bit.'

'Did Hollins agree?'

'Up to a point. He admitted that it had struck him as odd at the time, but on reflection he had come up with what he saw as the logical explanation. I have to tell you that this is where the anticlimax begins to creep in. Perhaps Toby would have made a better job of it, after all.'

'Never mind, go on about this logical explanation.'

'It had dawned on him that Mervyn must have been thinking of the weekday service, unaware, or having overlooked the fact, that the Sunday timetable would be greatly inferior. In order to satisfy himself on this point, he had verified it and, sure enough, on weekdays there was a fast through train to Paddington, departing at somewhere around the time they had arrived at the station. The sad thing, from your point of view and Matthew's too, to some extent, is that it could so easily be true.'

'And on the other hand it could equally well be true that by introducing this element of confusion and relying on Professor Hollin's practically guaranteed inability to tell Tuesday from Christmas Eve, Mervyn had been hoping to throw such a smokescreen around his movements that they could never finally be proved or disproved.'

'Possible, I daresay. Anyway, I'm relieved to hear that you're not too discouraged. Not that I subscribe to your theory of Mervyn having anything whatsoever to do with Barbara Landauer's murder, but it's a help to know that you'll have something to occupy your mind when you're no longer strutting around in a silly hat from seven thirty till eleven six nights a week.'

'Not to mention matinées. I don't think I shall be subscribing to it myself much longer, to be honest. Somehow or other, with all his faults, I can't see Mervyn getting into a pickle like that. All the same, there is something not quite natural about him at the moment and I wouldn't half mind finding out what brought it on.'

'So you really do mean to battle on?'

'I don't see why not, Robin, do you? Specially now he's made the first move. And, after all, we still have the small problem of Jimmie Peacock and his new affluence to sort out.'

16

The tea service was Rockingham china, dutifully and enthusiastically admired by Lorraine, for whose benefit it had no doubt been brought out, but the tea, when it came trickling from the Georgian silver pot, looked as though it had been made from chopped hay and appearances were not deceptive. The rock buns, however, were worthy of their name and the texture of the walnut cake suggested that it had been buried twenty years ago and dug up that afternoon, the whole being presided over by Mrs Houghton, wearing a hat of the same period.

She and I were left together when this feast was over, while Mervyn took Lorraine on a tour of the converted barn which housed his butterfly collection.

Matters fell out in this way by virtue of the fact that, earlier in the day, Robin had earned my undying gratitude for the second time that week. I no longer recall what the first act of sacrifice or heroism had been, but on Sunday morning he had offered to provide Beverly with police protection that afternoon by taking her to the golf course and teaching her the rudiments of the game, not to be deflected from this noble purpose even by Toby's warning that, if her golf matched up to her croquet, it would end by his being expelled from the club.

Knowing Mrs Houghton's preference for delivering lectures, as opposed to the give and take of social chatter, I provided her with an opening by saying:

'Mervyn tells me you're a JP. I've never been quite sure what that involved, but I imagine you must find it very arduous and demanding?'

136

'No, not at all,' she replied, grasping the opportunity without hesitation. 'I see it as my duty to serve the community in whatever way I am best fitted.'

'I realise that, but some people find that even the performance of their duty can be taxing at times.'

'Nonsense. That may be true of your generation, I daresay it is. Most young people seem to take the attitude nowadays that unless a job is ridiculously overpaid it isn't worth doing. Self first, self second, and self last, seems to be the motto. But we of the old school were brought up differently and we had traditions to live up to. Heaven only knows what will become of this country when we've all gone.'

'Although I suppose there have been one or two compensations along the way?'

'Compensations? What are you talking about, girl? I've never had any compensations and never expected them. I have simply done what I saw as my duty.'

'I was thinking that perhaps being on the Bench might have provided you with some rare and fascinating insights into human behaviour.'

'Dear me, no. That sort of romantic, highfalutin twaddle doesn't come into it. Facts are all that concern me. Find out whether they're guilty and then dole out the appropriate fine or punishment. We're dealing with juvenile delinquents, vandals and all those scum in our job, not psychopaths and perverts, thank the Lord.'

'Although some might say, I suppose, that without the proper treatment some of the minor scum might be destined to move on to worse deeds. There's a family in Toby's village, well, not a family exactly because the father died years ago, which may have some bearing on it, but anyway . . .'

'Bearing on what, may I ask?'

'The young man I'm talking about, who's in the minor scum league. I gather the father was quite a decent sort of man, so perhaps if he hadn't died young the son would have grown up to be quite decent, too.'

'Stuff and nonsense, my dear girl. People are either born wicked, or they're not. Broken homes and all that claptrap has nothing to do with it. You only have to look at Mervyn to know that. His father was killed before Mervyn was old enough to know him. It hasn't made him into a criminal.'

Refraining from passing on the news that there could be two opinions about that, I said:

'Well, of course, he had other advantages to make up for it, but what I wanted was your opinion about this: in the case of a young man, not brilliant, but not completely stupid either, who had drifted into a routine of petty thieving, how much would his chances depend on getting the right form of punishment from people like yourself? In other words, is he destined to be stuck in the same rut for ever, could he be pulled out of it and given a fresh start, or will he inevitably gravitate to more serious crimes and end up as major scum?'

'No good asking me. Some go one way, some another. Depends on the individual, I suppose. What's the name of this scallywag? Some local boy, you say, so I must have come across him.'

'I'm sure you have. His name is Jimmie Peacock.'

'Oh, Peacock! Yes, I know him only too well. He's the bane of our lives. Wouldn't do to say so, but sometimes I feel it would be a relief if he did get mixed up in something big and was sent down for a couple of years.'

'But you don't consider that likely?'

'Doubt it. He's got no ambition, even where crime is concerned. What's your interest in him?'

'None, personally, but he seems to be in trouble again and it made me wonder what eventually becomes of people like that.'

'Wasting your time. He's not worth it and you can forget all that sentimental twaddle about him being the victim of a one-parent upbringing. He's just a thoroughly bad lot and always has been. He may not have big ideas, but he's sly and he lies through his teeth every time he opens his mouth. If you take my advice, you'll steer well clear of him.'

It was interesting that she had not asked me what sort of trouble he was in now, which, since it consisted of nothing worse than a faint suspicion arising from his present life-style, was unlikely to have reached her ears. Perhaps more significantly still, the score was mounting. It was the second time in a week that a member of the Houghton clan had taken the trouble to warn me off.

Later that evening Robin and I returned to London, Lorraine and Beverly having gone ahead with Basil. If the Mystery Tour had gone according to schedule, the remaining members would be installed at the hotel before they arrived there, since they were due to check in between five and six o'clock.

Before leaving Roakes, Robin had taken Lorraine aside and tried for the second time to argue her out of her decision to expose Beverly to the risk of running into them. She had refused to be budged, though, insisting that it was essential for her to hand in her report to Virginia and that, furthermore, she would not be denied the chance to do so since it would contain no word of criticism about her charge, with whom two minutes' conversation would be enough to convince even the most sceptical of a miraculous transformation. Beverly was now as cheerful and amenable a girl as anyone could wish to see and Virginia was damn well going to see for herself.

In this, I had to admit she was justified, but Robin, more sceptical than most, had asked if she viewed the possibility of a chance encounter with Cornelius with equal complacency.

'Now don't be difficult, Robin. Why on earth should there be anything of the kind? Their plane leaves at nine in the morning, so the chances are a million to one against it. What we'll do is this. Soon as we get in we'll go straight to our suite, then call Virginia and Ed and invite them over. When you and Tessa arrive, we'll come down and meet you at the main entrance. Basil will be waiting outside and the four of us will go somewhere for dinner. The others will have left before she's even awake tomorrow, so what could go wrong? That is, you do have my room number written down, Tessa?'

'Yes, we should manage to run the New Westminster gauntlet this time. Are you really planning to take Basil back to New York with you?'

'Why not? He has his passport and he'll go to the Embassy tomorrow for a visa. Henry's going to love him. So, anyway, Robin, everything's taken care of and you can stop worrying. Besides . . .'

'Besides what?'

'I don't see there'd be such a hell of a lot to worry about if the two of them were to meet. She hasn't mentioned him once during these past few days and she certainly hasn't behaved like someone with a broken heart. Maybe she was only pretending to be serious about him, just a kind of game, really. And I over-reacted, as usual, wouldn't you know?'

'Nonsense!' I told her. 'The truth is that she's been having such a good time with you that it's been the holiday she really needed and all the silly goings-on were just to compensate for feeling secretly rather bored with trailing around looking at monuments to crime fiction. You did absolutely the right thing.'

'Thanks, Tessa, you're a brick, you both are. Two family-sized, gold-plated bricks and I'll see you this evening around seven, OK?'

'Looking forward to it,' Robin said, in the tone of one making an appointment with the hangman.

17

'I might have guessed,' he said at ten minutes past seven. 'We seem to have been here before.'

This was true in every sense because, having arrived at the New Westminster five minutes before the appointed time, our second visit was developing along depressingly similar lines to the first one.

This time there had been no delay in establishing contact with Lorraine, but instead of the reception clerk's announcement of our arrival being followed by his telling us that the ladies would be down in a jiffy, or as many jiffies as it took them to fight their way through the chaos of the lift service, there appeared to be a major hitch.

At the end of a one-sided conversation, the clerk being confined to almost total silence while Lorraine quacked away on the other, we were requested to repair to the Arena Bar, where Mrs Thurloe proposed to join us in due course.

'Where the hell's the Arena Bar, do you suppose?' Robin asked.

'Probably that open space which Lorraine calls the circus ring. Come on, we can at least get a drink to settle our nerves.'

The clientele was small that evening. Perhaps all the American tourists were avoiding the Arena Bar for fear of running into American tourists, or perhaps because, by a stroke of luck, it was the pianist's night off. I was especially thankful for this because Robin has a horror of saloon-bar pianists, not simply because of the noise they make, but because he is terrified of being asked to name his favourite tune. This had happened to him on one never-to-be-forgotten occasion and, in desperation, he had muttered the first title that came into his head, for the very good reason that it happened to be the one which had just been played.

In the absence of threats of that nature and, having fortified himself with a genuine, straight-up American dry martini, he began to relax in a truly miraculous fashion. Halfway through the second we had almost forgotten the reason for our presence there when, glancing sideways, I saw a tall, sandy-haired man advancing towards us.

'I trust I'm not interrupting anything?' he asked, inclining his head to within an inch of my extended hand, 'but I wondered whether I might join you for two minutes?'

'Yes, of course, do sit down. This is Colin Gascoine, Robin. I expect you remember Lorraine telling us about him?'

He looked uncertain whether he did or not, which was understandable, this being the first time the name had been mentioned in his hearing, but he overcame the problem by asking Colin what he was drinking.

'Oh, thanks very much. That looks like a good brew you're both on. I'll have the same, if I may.'

'Have you seen Lorraine?' I asked him, while Robin was going through the business of ordering it.

'Lorraine? Is she around? I haven't seen anyone, to tell you the truth. We didn't get in until after four and, what with sorting my flock into their right pens and dealing with sundry complaints about missing bath towels and faulty television sets, I haven't had time to unpack my bags yet.'

'Perhaps I should warn you, then, that you may be seeing her at any minute.'

'Why's that? Is she ... Oh Lord, you don't mean they're staying here?'

'Yes, but nothing to worry about. As soon as they turn up Robin and I will be taking them out to dinner and by the time they get back all the pens will be shut for the night.'

Colin did not look particularly reassured by this.

142

'That explains it, I suppose,' he muttered, apparently to himself, and then with a change of tone, 'My word, this is strong stuff. Just what I needed.'

'You've had a trying few days, by the sound of it,' Robin suggested.

'Oh, about average, on the whole. Mrs Dearing, who tells me she met you both on the first evening here, had a nasty turn, not serious, but a bit of a worry, as you can imagine.'

'Not another heart attack?' I asked.

''Fraid so. Only a minor spasm fortunately and she seemed all right the next morning, but, one way and another and good soul that she is, I'll be relieved to see her safely on that plane at nine o'clock tomorrow morning. Look, though, since we're liable to be interrupted at any minute, perhaps I should get down to business? I have news for you, Tessa. Won't go into it now, but I'd planned to drop in on you around tennish, on my way home tomorrow morning. Then I saw you both sitting up here and it seemed a good chance to ask you whether that would suit you all right.'

'Yes, fine. Is it about Barbara Landauer?'

'Right, and I think you'll be interested.'

'I'm sure I will. Who did you get it from?'

'Ginsberg, no less. He and his daughter joined us for our last day in Cambridge and after dinner I was invited up for a little informal chat. It was only partly informal, as it happens, and not all a waste of time from your point of view.'

'Can't you tell us about it now? It is bound to interest Robin quite as much as it does me,' I said, putting on the special expression which is meant to convey to Robin that on no account should he contradict me and that I would explain the slight deviation from the truth on some future occasion, 'That is, if you have no particular objection to being found here by Lorraine and Beverly, if they should turn up?'

'No, not really. Lorraine will always rank as one of my most memorable and favourite travelling companions and my relationship with Beverly has mellowed considerably after that

143

stunning evening you laid on for us at the theatre. Quite one of the brightest spots of the whole tour – for almost all of them, I might add.'

'Thank you,' I replied, curbing the impulse to enquire who the dissenters had been.

'Well, to get back to the subject of Mrs Landauer, I'll just give you the bones of what I learned yesterday and fill in some names and details I've jotted down when I see you tomorrow. It seems that blackmail was the name of her particular game . . .'

'Go on!' I said, 'I'm all ears.'

A moment later, however, they had to be switched to a new sound which he had already picked up himself. This was the voice of a page chanting out the incantation: 'Mr Gaskell telephone please', which he repeated at intervals of two or three seconds, his voice gradually fading away and then growing louder again as he made one entire circuit of the ground floor.

'Oh Lord, I bet he means me,' Colin said, getting up with a resigned expression. 'It's probably my wife. She was going to call me some time this evening. On the other hand, it could also be one of the flock who's mislaid a piece of luggage, or can't find the lightswitch. Sorry about that, but I'll be back if I get the chance and if you're still on your own. And thanks very much for the drink, by the way. It's done me a power of good.'

Perhaps he would have been all the better for a second one because when we next saw him, a few minutes later, he was walking rapidly towards the lifts which were in a side alley, whose entrance was directly opposite our table. He did not glance in our direction, but spent the interval while waiting for a lift in moving methodically from one to the next, pushing each button in turn.

He was rewarded at last and apparently too preoccupied to notice that Lorraine was among those who emerged from it. However, the lapse may have been on her side too, for she was looking just as worried and preoccupied herself. She was also on her own and stood gazing vacantly around, until attracted at last by the four waving hands from the dais. Instead of obeying

144

their signal, however, she went into a semaphore of her own, pointing first up to the ceiling and then to the lift lobby, before turning round and marching back to her point of entry.

'I tell you what,' Robin said. 'You go and find out what it's all about and I'll wait here.'

'You'll do no such thing,' I told him. 'If, as I strongly suspect, Beverly has done another bolt, no amount of clucking and tutting from me is going to help. Lorraine will need you far more than she does me.'

Explanations were forthcoming during the upward journey and the long trudge down what appeared to be the identical corridor we had trodden on our first visit.

'You couldn't exactly call it bolting,' Lorraine began by saying, 'because she came back.'

'So why the panic?'

'I thought you'd be wondering what had happened to us, that's why. You shouldn't seriously expect a girl like Beverly to have any idea of time, but I was angry and scared when I found she'd gone and I was getting worse with every second she didn't come back. It was stupid of me, I guess, but I felt so frustrated, sitting there all by myself and thinking that all the hard work I'd put in had been just a waste of time.'

'Exactly how and when did she get away, though?' Robin asked.

'We'd been to the Hayward Gallery, they have a special exhibition there which Henry wanted me to look at, and we had to walk about ten miles before we found a cab. So I told Bev I would lie down for half an hour and then take a shower. It wasn't much after five then, so we had plenty of time, and I advised her to do the same and reminded her to put on her finery, as we were going to dinner with you and Tessa. We'd already called in on Virginia and Ed, so that was all taken care of, and all we had to do was get ourselves together and look forward to the evening.'

'Did she take your advice?'

'I guess not. I must have dozed off because when I looked at my watch it was twenty after six and there was this note on my dresser.'

'How did she get into your room?' I asked. 'Don't tell me this is another of those hotels which hands out keys to anyone who chances to ask for them?'

'She didn't need a key, we have connecting rooms. It's the same as I had before, only with two bedrooms. That way, I can keep an eye on her. In theory, anyway. It doesn't work out so well when I take a nap for twenty minutes.'

'What did the note say?'

'That she'd gone to say goodbye to Edith Dearing. She'd found out her room number and she wouldn't be gone more than fifteen minutes.'

'Well, that doesn't sound bad. It was her last chance, after all, and I daresay she'd become quite attached to the old lady.'

'Oh, sure. Only problem was I had no way of telling how long the note had been there.'

'But of course, being you, you had to give her the benefit of the doubt,' Robin said, 'and hang on for the full fourteen and a half minutes. Did she repay you?'

'No.'

'In which case, your next move, presumably, was to find out Mrs Dearing's room number yourself and put through a call to enquire whether she happened to have seen Beverly lately.'

'Well, yes, I did get as far as the first part, as it happens, but then I thought I should put off the rest of it for just a short while. I'd based my whole relationship with her on mutual trust and the last thing I wanted now was for her to get the idea I was spying on her.'

'So you went on giving her just another five minutes until she did come back?'

'Right.'

'And how was she?' I asked, joining in the interrogation at this point. 'Apologetic? Defiant? Or unconcerned?'

'Just about all three of those in turn. Defensive, I guess, is the

146

best way to describe it. She looked really terrible, too, as though she'd been crying a lot, or meant to start crying any minute. I tried my hardest not to show how angry I felt, but, as acts go, it can't have been all that convincing because she kept telling me there was no need to be so tensed up because she could be in and out of the shower in ten minutes. She used up more time saying it than it would have needed to do it. Anyway,' Lorraine went on, scrabbling about in her bag for the plastic card, 'you'll be able to judge for yourselves if I can just get this damn thing the right way up.'

'I wonder?' Robin said.

'OK, you try it then. Men are always cleverer about this kind of thing.'

'I was wondering whether, in fact, we shall get a chance to judge for ourselves. Wasn't it rather risky to leave her on her own? Why are you so sure she won't have bolted again the minute your back was turned?'

'Don't worry, I've fixed her this time. I waited till she was under the shower, then I swiped all the towels and stashed them away in my closet. Even Houdini would have been stuck for a way out of that.'

Beverly may have missed her vocation, however, for we found her seated at Lorraine's dressing table, wrapped in a pink-and-white tweed coat, with a price-tag hanging out at the back. She was applying purple varnish to her nails, which didn't tone very well with her tanned freckly hands.

'Hi, everyone!' she called, flapping them up and down. 'I borrowed your coat, Lorraine, the one you bought yesterday. Hope it's OK?'

'Well, yes, I guess so. Don't you have a coat of your own?'

'Not as cosy as this and I was frozen stiff. They hadn't put one single towel out in the bathroom. Would you believe that? Not one. I could have died of pneumonia.'

I could tell from Lorraine's expression that she would not have regarded this outcome as any great cause for grief, although as a rule possessions were the last thing to arouse strong passions in her. She explained this departure from the norm by saying:

'Well, the only problem is, Bev, I bought that coat to take home for my friend, Sally. She's been having a hard time lately and she'd set her heart on a pink-and-white tweed from London and it was just her size and everything. I doubt I'll be able to replace it.'

'Oh, don't fuss so, Lorraine, you don't have to replace it. This'll dry out, if I just hang it overnight.'

'Maybe it will, but I'm not sure Sally will like all those purple blobs down the front. Hanging it up won't bring them out. Oh, excuse me, Robin ... Tessa, how about a drink? There's champagne on ice, or whatever you want.'

'I shall play safe with a martini, thank you,' Robin answered, 'and so will Tessa, if she knows what's good for her. How about you?'

'The same, and you're the only man east of Long Island Sound I'd trust to make them, so please go ahead.'

'I'm going to have champagne,' Beverly announced. 'It's ages and ages since I drank champagne.'

'Whatever you say, but wait until you're dressed, why not? Just run and put some clothes on and we'll have it ready for you when you come back.'

'If that's what you call defensive,' I remarked, 'I should hate to see her when she's on the aggressive.'

'Oh, that was just an act for your benefit. I like to think she doesn't bother to do it for me any more.'

'Were we meant to be impressed?'

'Well, no, that doesn't exactly fit either.'

'What Lorraine means, perhaps,' Robin suggested, 'is that the belligerence was a cover-up. It was concealing some other emotion.'

If Henry himself had uttered these words, she could not have looked more awestruck.

'You're brilliant, you know that, Robin? It was precisely what I was trying to say and I have to tell you I don't like it.'

'What other emotion?' I asked.

'Fear would be the main one, I'd say, but in some way I can't explain she struck me as more scared of herself than anything else.'

'Scared she was going dotty again?'

'That's how it looked from here. It was the way she behaved when she lost her camera and it was even more noticeable after the shoplifting. Almost like she knew she must have done it, without realising, and that could only mean she was losing her mind again and liable to do some other crazy, stupid thing at any time.'

'It can't be as simple as that, surely?' Robin asked.

'What's simple about it? And why not?'

'Because there's a common denominator here, which you seem to have overlooked. Both the incidents you've referred to occurred when you and Beverly were still part of the organised tour, whereas you assure us that all has been plain sailing on a placid sea ever since you formed yourselves into a splinter group. However, today has brought two changes in that pattern. The first is that Beverly has reverted to her bad old ways and the second ... well, you don't need to be told what the second is.'

'No,' Lorraine admitted, 'even I don't need to have that spelt out for me. What it amounts to is that I've blown it again. I should have listened to your warning voice and kept well clear of the New Westminster, so long as there was any risk of her meeting up with the old gang. Honestly though, Robin, I've not trying to shift the blame, but I was concentrating on Virginia and Ed and the importance of stuffing their little heads with the right kind of messages to carry home to Lynn. How was I to know just a few hours under the same roof could lead to this? Do you imagine they've been secretly keeping in touch all this while, with me preening myself on having made her forget all about him?'

'You refer to Cornelius, I take it?'

'Who else?'

'But it was Mrs Dearing she went to call on this evening and I can't see her conniving in any kind of deception. Or perhaps you believe that Mrs Dearing knew nothing whatever about it and Beverly never went near her? If so, why not pick up the telephone and ask her?'

The question was answered by a disembodied voice from the shadows beyond the room.

'You can't pick up the telephone and ask her,' Beverly said, slowly materialising in the doorway, 'because Mrs Dearing is dead.'

She then tottered a few steps further into the room, swayed sideways, righted herself, fell forward and collapsed unconscious on to the sofa.

'Is it a genuine faint, or is she faking?' I asked Robin a few minutes later, while Lorraine continued to hover round Beverly, begging her to open her eyes and dousing her chin with brandy.

'Could be either.'

'She seems to be taking an unnaturally long time to come out of it.'

'Yes, I know, but her pulse is all right, a bit erratic but nothing to speak of and she's breathing quite normally.'

'So you do think it's put on?'

'Not necessarily. I'd say it's more likely that she's asleep.'

'Honestly, Robin, that beats everything! How could anyone doze off at a moment like this?'

'I know it sounds daft, but I came across a chap once who used to drop off regularly as soon as the bombs started falling. He couldn't help himself, it was because he was terrified. A form of hysteria, or self-hypnosis. Necrolepsy, or something like that, is the scientific term, I believe, but Nature, by any other name, can be a wonderful healer.'

'We must get a doctor,' Lorraine moaned. 'For God's sake, what are we all doing, standing around like this when what we need is a doctor? Could you see to it right away, Robin? I know they have one on call.'

'I will, if you insist,' he replied, 'but don't you feel, in these rather peculiar circumstances, it could lead to even worse trouble?'

'Well, yes, I know what you mean, but there's just no alternative. We can't simply sit here and pray. She could have a heart attack, concussion, anything.'

'I doubt it. Her heart seems in good shape and you can't concuss yourself on an upholstered sofa. If you'll just bear with me for a while, I suggest we move her on to her own bed and let her sleep it out. I promise you she'll come to no harm. She's had a bad shock, I believe, and the best thing would be to leave her to recover from it in her own way.'

Accustomed as she was to male domination in all emergencies, Lorraine gave in with scarcely a quibble and her faith was not misplaced. Before the hour was out Beverly had opened her eyes, sat up in bed and started to complain about being hungry. Luckily, this presented no problem because Lorraine, with all the ruthlessness which the mere fact of identifying herself as Mrs Henry Thurloe always gave her, had already bludgeoned the restaurant manager into despatching his underlings to suite Number 602 with a trolley laden with soup, sandwiches and exotic fruit. Taking her cue from Robin, she made no mention to Beverly of the events which had made this necessary, but set about dishing up a dainty three-course supper, which the invalid wolfed down with evident relish.

Before this stage was reached, however, each of us had done a twenty-minute solitary stint in Beverly's bedroom, with me volunteering to go first, when I considered the chances of her either waking up or dying would be at their lowest. Lorraine then took over and when I rejoined Robin I asked him what they had been talking about during my absence.

'Tell you later. I'm going downstairs for a few minutes.'

'What for?'

'I'll tell you that later too. Don't let anyone in unless they knock three times and say they're me.'

So there I was, floating about in yet another vacuum, having

151

already read all three books on the bedside table and with nothing whatever to do except make a brief inspection of the bottles and jars and contents of the wardrobe, under the stern and disapproving eye of Henry, whose photographs were dotted about in various strategic points of the room.

Fifteen minutes passed in this way and I was toying with the idea of experimenting with Lorraine's nail varnish when Robin returned.

'You have one or two things to tell me,' I reminded him.

'So I have. You wanted to know what Lorraine and I had been talking about.'

'Among other things.'

'We were discussing the merits and otherwise of investigating the truth of Beverly's statement concerning the death of Mrs Dearing. She was all for the direct approach.'

'Whereas you took a more cautious line?'

'I pointed out that the upshot would most likely be inconclusive, but could also lead to precisely the sort of complications she was hoping to avoid. There was no particular reason to suppose she would find Mrs Dearing in her room at eight o'clock in the evening and, if she were not, it did not follow that she was dead. On the other hand, if Beverly had got her facts right, which is always open to question, to enlist an outsider's help in finding out the truth could end with her being landed with more questions than answers.'

'And did she see the sense of that?'

'In the end. I told her it was just the kind of advice she would be likely to get from an experienced lawyer and that did it.'

'Although, of course, even if Edith is dead, there is no reason to assume that she has been murdered, is there?'

'None at all.'

'All the same, I'd awfully like to know whether she is or not, wouldn't you?'

'I admit to a certain curiosity on the subject, yes.'

'So what were you doing downstairs?'

'Trying to find out whether she is or not, of course. What else?'

'Oh, Robin, you really can be maddening when you put your mind to it. Did you succeed?'

'I think so.'

'So what the hell have we been talking about for the past five minutes?'

'I said I thought so. I couldn't claim to have proved it. And, if I'm wrong, of course, the fog surrounding this subject becomes even thicker.'

'You're making it thicker with every word you utter. Do come to the point.'

'I took the lift down to the garage, which, as you may know, is in the basement. From there I walked up to street level and re-entered by the main door. It happened to be a relatively quiet period and I managed to grab the attention of a reception clerk who was unable to sustain the pretence of having more important things to do.'

'And, having grabbed it, you asked to see Mrs Dearing?'

'Certainly not. It might have landed me into doing exactly that and heaven knows what we should have found to say to each other.'

'Quite a lot, judging by the way you're going on at the moment. So what did you do?'

'I asked her to find out whether there was a lady of that name staying in the hotel. I could be mistaken, of course, but if there was I should like to leave a note for her.'

'Oh, very cunning! And what was the upshot?'

'It was some time in coming. She said she was unable to tell me offhand, but would go into the back office and consult the card index file. That was a step forward, of course.'

'I don't see why.'

'Surely even a moderately well run hotel would keep that kind of information handy at all times? In normal circumstances, it could hardly involve anything so cumbersome as searching through files.'

'And what came of it when she'd done that?'

'The news that there had been a Mrs Dearing staying there, but she had checked out a few hours ago. I daresay that was accurate, as far as it went, but she omitted to add whether or not the lady had left by the service lift, en route to the morgue.'

'And you really think that's likely?'

'Well, it's hard to believe she could have left under her own steam. Since we know for a fact that she only arrived a few hours ago, it would have required her to enter the building, take a quick look round and go straight out again. Understandable, if it had been you or me, but hardly practical for an elderly woman, confined to a wheelchair and with an early plane to catch in the morning.'

'So what's next?'

'Wait and see, I suppose. There's nothing any of us can do, at any rate until Prince Charming turns up and wakens our sleeping princess. It begins to sound as though she knew what she was talking about, but, as you say, there's no reason to assume it wasn't a natural death. In fact, I seem to remember your friend Colin saying there'd been another mild heart attack only the other day. Nothing particularly sensational about it if she'd had another this evening, which finished her off.'

'Although it wouldn't surprise me, either, to learn that she possessed some knowledge which could have been damaging to someone else. Nor would I be stunned out of my wits to discover that Beverly has a good idea who it was. Still, speculation of that kind is a waste of time at this stage. Are you going to tell Lorraine what you have found out, so far?'

'She ought to know, don't you think? It will then be up to her to decide how to proceed, but I shall have to leave the telling of it to you. It's me next for the minder's chair and, judging by noises off, my time has now arrived.'

It did not take long in the telling and Lorraine received the news with relative calm. Having kept a close watch on Beverly throughout the twenty minutes, monitoring her breathing and pulse, she was now convinced that, incredible as it had sounded, Robin had been right. The poor child was suffering from shock and this was Nature's way of dealing with it. Nor

154

was she in any mood to be cast down by my veiled hints that the shock might have been too severe to be erased entirely by an hour's sleep and, furthermore, that there could still be a few shocks in store for the rest of us.

So I kept these forebodings to myself and asked instead whether she had ever found out what Ed had done with the yellow string glove.

'Certainly, I did,' she replied, 'and I'd been meaning to tell you. He still has it.'

'Good for him! Did he tell you why he hadn't returned it to the owner, or handed it in at the desk?'

'The answer may surprise you. He said he had decided that the smart thing would be to hang on to it, in case Cornelius tried any more funny business and it came to a confrontation. He still hasn't said anything to Virginia, though. He didn't want her to get the idea of having a private confrontation, all of her own.'

'You know, Lorraine, I'm beginning to believe we've under-estimated Ed. Anyone with his looks ought by rights to be solid bone all the way up, just to even the score, but he seems to have a lot more sense than that conceited wife of his.'

'Oh, Virginia's not a bad girl, deep down. Just spoilt, that's her trouble. Being the first-born, as well as the beauty, naturally she was always Earl's own little girl and he never made any secret of it. Poor Bev has always been second-best and well she knew it.'

I was interested by these observations, but there was no time to ask her to elaborate on them because only a few seconds later we were joined by Robin, who informed us that the patient was sitting up and clamouring for nourishment.

'You didn't have to sit it out for long,' I remarked, as Lorraine busied herself with this matter. 'Did you cheat and stick a few pins in her, by any chance?'

'Not exactly, I noticed some stirrings of life, so I decided to play God.'

'What fun for you! Good performance?'

'Pretty good. I said in clear and godlike tones: "OK,

Beverly, the demons have all gone away now. It is time to wake up."'

'You should try it more often. How is she now?' I asked Lorraine, who had come in to collect the second course. 'Apart from hungry?'

'She seems fine. All set to spend the rest of the evening watching some trash on television. I don't understand her at all. Not a word about passing out, or Edith, and all the things we've been worrying about. Think I ought to jog her memory?'

'I'd leave her alone if I were you,' Robin advised. 'Let her take her own time. There can't be much cause for alarm now. We'd have heard, if there were.'

'How would we have heard?'

'Well, assuming Edith has died and Beverly was with her, she wouldn't simply be able to drift away and forget about it. She'd be needed for all sorts of reasons.'

'How about if no one knew she was there?'

'In that case, we'd have even less to worry about, wouldn't you say? And, if there's nothing more we can do just now, I think it's time for us to drift away. We'll be at home, if you need us.'

'But before we go,' I said, taking a piece of paper from my bag, 'next time you call Henry, which I imagine will be in about five minutes from now, there's something I'd like him to set his spies on to. I've written it down for you.'

When she had read it she looked up and glowered at me:

'Are you certain about this, Tessa?'

'Oh yes, pretty certain,' I replied. 'After all, I had it from the horse's mouth.'

'You sounded very sanguine,' I remarked, as we set forth at last on the journey home, starting with the long walk down the corridor to the lifts. 'Were you just saying all that to cheer her up, or because you were aching to leave?'

'A bit of both, although it wasn't altogether insincere. If Beverly does know something which could be dangerous to someone else, or embarrassing to herself, she's unlikely to confess to it on demand and, anyway, the chances are that she doesn't. I should say that the most likely explanation is that she knocked on Mrs Dearing's door, which was opened by Marilou, who told her to go away because her aunt had been taken ill and was about to leave by ambulance for the hospital. Naturally, that would be too tame a story to appeal to Beverly. She had to jazz it up a bit and, having done so, found herself in a situation she couldn't get out of. Hence the refreshing sleep, followed by comforting amnesia when she woke up.'

'I expect you're right as usual, Robin, but all the same I can't wait to find out whether Edith really is dead and, if so, who was with her at the time.'

'I daresay you won't have long to wait. I may be able to do some unofficial fishing in that pool and bring you home a minnow or two for lunch.'

'Unless I've beaten you to it.'

'How come?'

'Through Colin Gascoine. He's bound to know all about it. In fact, I've realised since that it must have been the subject of that telephone call which sent him scurrying off to the lift just after he left us and you may have heard him say that he proposes to call on me in Oxford tomorrow morning?'

'I did indeed, and I have to say that I thought you'd gone bonkers. Can you really have forgotten that your run at Oxford has ended?'

'Of course not, but I still have some remnants of packing to do and some stuff to collect from the theatre some time or other and it's obvious that he wants to start his journey home as soon as he's seen them off at the airport. He might not have been so keen if it had meant coming back to London to see me. I'll leave early and take the car this time, which means I can be back for lunch, if you really feel like dropping in for a snack.'

'Oh, very handsome of you, I must say!' Robin replied with most uncharacteristic sarcasm. 'And I'll certainly make a point of telephoning in advance to find out if it's convenient. A snack indeed! I might have been planning to drop in for a three-course lunch, for all you know.'

I did not remind him of the many three-course dinners which had withered away, owing to the last-minute news that he would not, after all, be home until midnight. It was clear that something had really annoyed him and there was also the bare chance he would have retorted by reminding me that such lapses had occurred in the call of duty, which could hardly be claimed as my motive for haring off to Oxford for a chat with Colin Gascoine.

18

It was as well that I had exercised restraint because by twelve
fifteen it had become evident that even a snack would have
been beyond my powers to provide. Having arrived in Oxford
soon after ten and gone to my room to finish the packing, I rang
the reception desk to say that I was expecting Mr Gascoine and
wished to be informed the minute he arrived.

Nearly an hour went by before it occurred to me that the bar
was now open and that he might be waiting for me there. It was
not so, however, and neither was he in the coffee lounge or any
of the other public rooms.

My main reaction at this point was one of annoyance that my
early start from London had been unnecessary, and it was not
until after I returned from collecting my odds and ends from the
theatre that I realised something so serious must have occurred
as to have made it impossible for him either to turn up in person
or to send me a message. Having reached this conclusion the
voice in my head, which had been hinting what this might
signify ever since Beverly's dramatic collapse, became so strong
and insistent that I went straight upstairs to my room again and
put through a call to London, a matter in which I considered
there was now not a moment to be lost.

As it turned out, though, quite a lot of moments were lost,
due to the vagaries of the management and staff of the New
Westminster Hotel, whose teething troubles seemed to extend
right down to the gums and roots.

The telephone was answered on the second ring by a
cheerful-sounding female, who wished me good morning and

asked if she could help me. I told her in five words how she could and was requested to hold the line. During the interval which ensued I completed four words in the crossword puzzle and was starting on the fifth when a man's voice came on the line and asked if he could help me.

I repeated my request, waited again and had almost reached the point of flinging the telephone across the room in my rage and frustration, as I pictured my quarry slipping away beyond my grasp, when the baton was picked up by yet another female voice. This brought me to within a millimetre of telling its owner in the most fanciful terms exactly how she could help me, but I checked myself in the nick of time, as it dawned on me that her question had actually been 'Who is this?'

It happens to be a phrase which, in that context, I have often complained about to Lorraine, for I consider it appropriate only from someone who comes from behind and covers your eyes with his hands, but this time I gave my name and asked in dulcet tones whether it would be convenient to speak to Mr Ginsberg.

'I'm sorry, he's not here right now. Would you care to leave a message?'

'I'd rather talk to him some time, if it's possible. Do you know when he'll be back?'

This was followed by a muffled gabble, as, with her hand partially covering the mouthpiece, the telephonist relayed the news to the absent Mr Ginsberg. Then, addressing me again, she asked:

'You did say you were Theresa Crichton?'

'Yes.'

Another pause and then: 'My father has just come in. He'll be glad to talk to you.'

He had a slow, amiable-sounding voice, which was reassuring, as were his opening words:

'Good afternoon, young lady. What may I do for you?'

'Oh, is it afternoon already? My goodness!'

'Three minutes after. Is that what you called to ask me?'

160

'No, I wondered if I might come and see you some time this ... evening?'

'Why not?'

'That's extremely kind of you, Mr Ginsberg. Would five o'clock suit you?'

'I'll be here. Room 482. Come right on up.'

'Are you always so courteous to perfect strangers?'

'Oh, you're no stranger, Miss Crichton. Perfect, maybe, but no stranger to me and my daughter.'

'Really? We've never met, surely?'

'No, but I've been hearing about you from several people, when we were over at Cambridge a few days ago.'

It would have been gratifying, in one sense, if the explanation had been that they had seen me too often on the screen to think of me as a stranger, but, all things considered, the one he had given me was even more propitious.

I had toyed with the idea of asking Mr Ginsberg to reconnect me with the switchboard, but on reflection decided that this was probably a far too complicated manoeuvre for the New Westminster to cope with and that I should leave Lorraine and Beverly on ice for the time being and deal with the domestic front first. That meant a call to Beacon Square to ask Mrs Cheeseman to tell Robin, should he ring up, that I had been delayed in Oxford and would not be home until after six. I was tempted to add that I might be the bearer of hot news, but this might have been too complicated for Mrs Cheeseman to cope with and had to be abandoned too.

Mr Ginsberg was alone when I presented myself in Room 482, his daughter, as he explained, having not yet returned from a visit with an old schoolfriend, who was married, as so many American daughters' schoolfriends nowadays seem to be, to a British politician.

He was a stout, friendly mannered man, very clean and cosy-looking, like a well-groomed, silver-haired teddy bear,

161

and he came straight to the point. The only snag was that his point bore no resemblance to mine.

It appeared that he had been much impressed by the many favourable comments he had received from members of the Mystery Readers' Tour about their visit to the theatre in Oxford and of the privilege they had enjoyed of meeting and talking with members of the cast, thereby getting a peep behind the scenes, as it were.

This had convinced him that there was a market for something in the generalised area of a Theatre Buffs' Tour, which could be included in future schedules, and he could already picture the applications pouring in. There need be no limit to its popular appeal and potentialities, providing . . .

'Providing what?'

'We can get the right kind of liaison set up over here. Everything would depend on that. No use leaving it to one of the run-of-the-mill tour operators to handle. It would need co-operation with someone on the inside who was personally familiar with the background.'

'You're not by any chance offering me the job of courier, Mr Ginsberg?'

This suggestion provoked gales of merry laughter but had not, it appeared, been so wide of the mark. What, in fact, he proposed was that I, in return for a hefty fee, should become advisory consultant to his firm, with the function of arranging on each of these 'specialty tours' for the clients to have the entrée into a West End theatre, there to sit in at a rehearsal and be conducted backstage afterwards, to meet and talk with the cast and production staff.

The idea of taking part in such a fairy-tale scheme was so ludicrous as almost to make me laugh aloud, but I pretended to take it seriously, hoping in this way to create a favourable climate in which to move by easy stages to some enquiries of my own on another subject.

So, under the guise of seeking more information as to what would be required of me, I began by questioning him about the travel business in general, registering stunned amazement on learning how much more complex and fascinating it was than the layman could ever conceive and, when this had the desired effect, I edged my way forward and sideways into particular aspects, including names and personalities.

The system worked, as it often does, and so free, frank and forthright did our conversation become that, with scarcely any trouble at all, it seemed quite natural to introduce the subject of Barbara Landauer.

'Did you ever meet her?' I asked.

'Why yes, at one time and another. I guess there weren't many of us in New York who didn't have that experience somewhere along the line.'

'People such as yourself, with money and influence, you mean?'

'You could say that. Matter of fact, I may have known her a little more intimately than some of the others. She was on my payroll for a brief period.'

'Really? How fascinating! In what capacity?'

'I hired her to do a specialised job for me, for which her talents and experience appeared to be ideally suited.'

'But it didn't last long, you say? What went wrong? Had you over-estimated the talents and experience?'

'No, more a matter of integrity. It gradually became clear to me that she was in the double-agent category.'

'Not spying for Intourist, by any chance?'

'Not far off, young lady. It certainly came into the commercial espionage bracket.'

'How did you find out?'

'I had asked her to take on an investigative job for me. One or two disturbing rumours were beginning to circulate in certain quarters which, if true, would have indicated a systematic betrayal of confidence and posed a serious threat to my business reputation. I had formed an idea of who might be behind it, but had no way of pinning it on this person. Barbara had a number of connections, here and in Europe, which were not available to me and I asked her to use her discretion to find out what she could.'

'Instead of which, you found she was working for the other side?'

'Something like that. I heard, quite by chance, from a compatriot of yours whom I'd met in New York some months previously, when we were setting up a project, that she'd been seen around in the company of the very individual she'd been hired to investigate.'

'But wouldn't that have been the best way of finding out what he was up to?'

'In theory, I'd say you were right. In this case, in view of all the time and expense involved, the results were disappointingly negative. So either she was incompetent, or she was using the information to further her own ends. This is not the kind of question I would want to make a habit of asking about my employees, so she and I parted company.'

'And, from the sound of it, she must have made quite a few enemies in her time. No wonder the police are having such trouble digging out the one who became desperate enough to kill her. Well, I've taken up too much of your time already, so I'll say goodnight and thank you so much for the drink.'

'My pleasure, but haven't you forgotten something, young lady?'

'Have I?'

'You haven't told me why you came here this evening.'

I had been prepared for this question to come earlier in our conversation and had been inclined to congratulate myself as the minutes passed without its cropping up. Surprisingly enough, however, the timing enabled me to answer with no more or less than the plain truth and I said:

'Oh, nor I have. Isn't that stupid, but I've been so fascinated by what you've been telling me and I've learned so many new and interesting facts that it seems trivial in comparison. I just wondered whether you might have Colin Gascoine's private number?'

'No, I don't. I can give you the name of his firm, if that would help?'

'Well, no, I did think of that, but this is just a personal matter and he might not wish them to be involved.'

'A personal matter?'

'In a way. We'd become quite good friends during the tour and he had planned to drop in for a farewell drink with me in Oxford this morning, after he'd seen his party off at the airport. He didn't turn up and I wondered if anything had gone wrong.'

'No, I can assure you nothing at all had gone wrong, I would have been the first to hear if it had,' Mr Ginsberg replied firmly, thereby confirming my belief that any reference to such a disagreeable topic as one of the clients having dropped dead would have done my cause no good at all.

'Yes, I'm sure you would and I daresay I misunderstood him. Or perhaps he was in such a tearing hurry to get home to his wife and family that he forgot all about it. Never mind, it's not important.'

It struck me that Mr Ginsberg looked at me with a rather doubtful expression as he shook hands and saw me out, and his manner had become hesitant too. However, I hoped this merely indicated that he was wondering whether, after all, he had been too hasty in supposing me to be up to the high standard of alertness and efficiency which High and Wide Tours, Inc. required of its employees and consultants.

19

This interview had provided so much food for thought that once again I put off the business of tracking down Lorraine and getting the latest news from that front, in favour, this time, of going straight home and into a hot bath, which is the best recipe I know for clearing the head and planning the next move in the game.

However, this consummation also had to be postponed because when I arrived at Beacon Square, soon after six, Robin was already there and he told me that Lorraine and Beverly were on their way and might arrive any moment.

'Or more likely half an hour, I suppose,' he added, 'allowing for Lorraine's obstinate belief that there are five hundred seconds in every minute, plus the fact that they are doubtless coming with Basil instead of on foot.'

'We can't rely on it, though, so tell me as fast as you can what sort of faces we should wear for this occasion. First of all, what's the story behind the story of Edith Dearing?'

'Not unlike the one in front. She died from a heart attack.'

'Oh dear, I am sorry. I kept hoping it might not be true. She was such a dauntless old party. When was it exactly?'

'Yesterday evening, not earlier than six fifteen, not later than seven.'

'In other words, when you and I were tossing back dry martinis and waiting for Lorraine?'

'Who was upstairs waiting for Beverly.'

'Yes, although surely Beverly can't have been there when it happened? In fact, there can't have been anyone with her, otherwise why such vagueness about the time? So who found her?'

'Marilou. She'd been in her own room next door, getting ready for dinner, and she went in to help her aunt downstairs just before seven thirty, which was their invariable routine. And that, as you'll recall, can't have been so very long before Beverly returned and got hauled over the coals for keeping us all waiting.'

'Yes, you're right, although Marilou can't have known anything about that. I daresay she didn't even know that Lorraine and Beverly were under the same roof.'

'However, she did know that someone had been with her aunt just before she died.'

'How?'

'Two dirty tooth glasses and two miniature bottles from the refrigerator locker, both empty. One glass half filled with water, the other with dregs of tomato juice and vodka. Since Mrs Dearing was teetotal, it is safe to assume that her visitor was the vodka drinker and furthermore that he or she had stayed for more than just a few minutes. Even a hardened drinker would need time to polish off a double vodka.'

'How did you manage to find all this out?'

Just for a second Robin assumed the rather prim expression which usually indicates that he is searching for some polite words to tell me to mind my own business, but this time it passed and he said:

'From the doctor who arrived on the scene twenty minutes later. He, or one of his partners, is permanently on call and he happened to be the same one who turned up when she had her first attack. You remember that incident with the lift doors?'

'Perfectly.'

'Well, it seems that he gave her a pretty thorough going over on that occasion, along with some stern warnings and, from the notes he'd made at the time, it was evident that her heart was in such poor shape that something of this kind could have been expected at any time. The slightest shock or over-exertion would have been enough. That's why there was no bother in getting the death certificate.'

'Which could have been very convenient for someone.'

'Maybe, although I doubt if there'd have been much difficulty without him. Elderly woman who've suffered for years with chronic arthritis are probably always more prone to sudden heart failure than the rest of us and there are numerous witnesses to testify that Mrs Dearing was particularly vulnerable in that respect.'

'In fact, one could almost imagine the first episode being a kind of dress rehearsal for the real thing, in order to fix that point firmly in everyone's mind. However, that rather cuts across another theory which I've been gradually building all day. It needs thought.'

'And, in the meantime, perhaps you ought to set your subconscious to work on some total recall and ask it to remind you which of the touring party were vodka drinkers and which were not.'

'Well, not Beverly, as far as I know. Not Marilou, I'd be prepared to bet and certainly not Cornelius.'

'Which seems to point the finger of guilt squarely at one of them.'

'You mean the other way round, don't you? . . . Oh yes, I get it now.'

'One could hardly expect any self-respecting murderer to ignore such an obvious dodge as that.'

'Specially as he or she would only have needed to take a sip or two before administering the slight shock, or whatever, and then pull the plug on the rest of it. On the other hand, perhaps he was one jump ahead and it was a double-bluff? Anyway, there's no time for that now because I want to hear about Beverly. What did you gather?'

'Everything back to normal, for the time being at any rate. It seems that she was rather jumpy this morning, or suffering from the after-effects of champagne, maybe, so Lorraine dragged her

168

off on one of those river-steamer trips to Greenwich, which soon brought the sparkle back.'

'Oh, she enjoyed Greenwich, did she?'

'I can't tell you whether she did or not, or whether she actually noticed it. Once aboard, they fell in with a young American couple and it turned out that the wife was the sister-in-law, or second cousin or something, of one of Henry's junior partners. So, with those credentials, Lorraine lost no time in getting tickets for the four of them at Drury Lane this evening.'

'That's nice. What have they got there?'

'Some American musical, I forget which one. Will you explain why it is that the first thing all Americans do when they set foot in London is to hurry off and see some musical which has been running on Broadway for fourteen years.'

'Same reason as we hurry off to track down an English newspaper, I daresay. It takes some of the horror out of being abroad. Although, to be fair,' I added, as Robin got up to answer the doorbell, 'you may be sure that Lorraine has only let herself in for this jaunt out of a sense of duty. Henry would definitely look down his nose.'

'How about you, Beverly?' he enquired, having mixed Lorraine's drink to specifications. 'Gin and tonic? Bloody Mary?'

However, if she recognised the trap, she slid out of it and asked for campari on the rocks.

Five minutes later she put her glass down and interrupted Lorraine's flow of praise for the couple they had met on the river steamer to ask if I had any photographs of the show.

'Show?' I repeated. 'What show would that be?'

'Yours. The one we saw at Oxford.'

'Oh, that! You mean publicity stills?'

'Right. Do you have any?'

'One or two. Why do you ask?'

'I want to borrow them so I can get copies made.'

169

'There's no need for that, but what do you want them for?'

'My photographic records, to show my mother when I get home. I've made a collection of the entire trip, all but that one evening.'

'She wanted to sneak her camera into the theatre, would you believe?' Lorraine explained, 'but I told her we'd be thrown out.'

'And it wouldn't have been any use, if you had let me take it. We were sitting too far back. How about it, Tessa?'

'OK. They're in my desk upstairs. You'd better come and look through them and take your pick.'

'Unfortunately these are not the only missing pieces from your records, are they?' I asked, when she had whittled her choice down to three.

'Yes, they are, I have stacks and stacks of them.'

'How about the day you spent at Roakes, when you lost your camera?'

'It came back.'

'In a sense, but it wasn't the same one, was it? And so it didn't have the film inside.'

'Oh, you heard about that? Well, it wasn't important. I'd just put a new roll in and there were only four or five exposures used up.'

'Forgive my contradicting you, Beverly, but I consider it very important. It's my belief those four or five were taken on or near the Common.'

'I didn't go on the Common. I told you that.'

'I know, and you can go on telling me until you turn blue, but I still shan't believe you. Furthermore, I'm pretty certain that, whether you realise it or not, one of the shots you took showed the figure of a man who was lurking not far away from you and, in fact, was the one who nicked your camera.'

'How could anyone have done that? I was wearing it on a chain around my neck, like I always do.'

'Nevertheless, you lost it, didn't you? And my theory is that

170

you took it off and laid it on the ground because it got in your way when you bent down to pick some wildflowers which were growing on the Common. I also consider it likely that you became so engrossed in this task that you wandered further afield than you'd meant to and when you straightened up you saw someone, some distance away, who you thought you recognised. So, one way and another, your attention had been diverted for several minutes and when you went back to the spot where you remembered leaving your camera, it was no longer there. Am I right?'

'No, no, it's not true. ... Oh, leave me alone, can't you? You're making me confused.'

'Never mind, I've nearly done now, but I think the time has come to get this straightened out. There's one thing, you see, which has never been properly explained. When you arrived back at the house your dress was torn, your hair was in a tangle and your hand was scratched. No doubt, if you'd been asked, you'd have said it had happened when you were clambering about in the wild part of the garden and, no doubt also, Lorraine would have accepted that, but not me or Toby. He may refer to it as the wilderness in his fanciful moments, but the fact is, Mr Parkes prefers to keep his wildernesses tame. You wouldn't find many weeds there at any time of the year, far less ugly things like brambles and nettles. So I think it's time you dropped the pretence of never having set foot on the Common. The sooner you do, the sooner you'll be out of this mess it's landed you in.'

'What mess? I don't have any idea what you're talking about. I'm not in a mess, you must be crazy,' Beverly squeaked, looking quite terrified.

'Oh yes, you are. Some of the time you try to block it out of your mind and pretend it doesn't exist, but then back it comes and swallows you up again. That's when you start squeaking and looking terrified. And the sad thing is that none of it's your fault. That's why I'd like to try and help, if only you'd stop lying to me.'

171

'What do you . . . how do you know so much?' Beverly asked, beginning to waver at last, as, with a burst of mistiming which would have earned him a place in the *Guinness Book of Records,* Robin put his head round the door and said:

'Aren't you two ever coming down? Lorraine is starting to worry about Basil worrying about your being late for the theatre.'

'Oh gosh, yes, she's right,' Beverly gabbled, collecting up the photographs, and I knew that the moment of truth had come and gone.

I had not finished with her yet, however, and told Robin in a steely voice that we should be down just as soon as I'd found the right-sized envelope. Having done so, I said:

'Well, give it some thought, Beverly, and while you're about it, there are a couple of other things which might be worth remembering. One is that there's been another event in your life recently for which no pictorial record exists.'

She was trying to push the photographs into the envelope, making a clumsy job of it, and did not answer so I continued:

'All right, I'll remind you. I am speaking of the time when, but for the fortuitous intervention of your tour operator, you came within inches of being arrested for shoplifting.'

She was walking rapidly downstairs ahead of me by that time and we almost had a nasty collision because she stopped abruptly in her tracks and, turning sideways, ducked her head down between her hands, as they clutched the bannister.

'Yes, I do realise how rotten it must be but I think you have to face it, and my next one is going to sound even more disagreeable, I'm afraid. I'd like you to cast your mind back to that hideous moment when you walked in and found Mrs Dearing dead and try to remember whether or not she was wearing her diamond ring.'

20

'Who was the maniac who telephoned in the middle of the night?' were Robin's first words, when he arrived in my room with the post and newspapers the following morning.

'Not quite the middle. Just after midnight, to be precise.'

'And?'

'It was Beverly.'

'I suppose I might have known. What did she have to say that was so urgent it couldn't wait till a civilised hour? That she enjoyed the show?'

'No, she wanted to be sure of being able to see me before I went back to Oxford this morning.'

'But you're not going back to Oxford this morning.'

'You and I know that, but Beverly either didn't or had forgotten. Having put her right on that, I told her I was lunching with Toby at Roakes and she might as well come with me and we'd talk on the journey. In which case, she should be here punctually at ten because I have to pay a call on the way.'

'You didn't tell me you were lunching with Toby. When was that decided?'

'At about half past midnight, which was a bit too late to ring him up and, anyway, he wouldn't have answered. I'll see to it as soon as I've drunk my coffee. Why don't you join us?'

'Don't be fatuous.'

'It might do your friend, Sergeant Matthews, a bit of good.'

'You're being very smug and enigmatic, Tessa, and it's a bit too early in the morning for that kind of thing. Besides, I have to leave in a minute. Would you care to tell me in a few plain words what goes on?'

'Nothing much. Just that I feel I may be on the brink of finding the answer to all the puzzles surrounding the Mystery Readers' Tour, not to mention who murdered Barbara Landauer.'

There were no half measures with Beverly and, having made up her mind to confess all, all was what I got, as we bowled down the M4, crawled over Storhampton bridge and niggled our way through the winding lanes to Roakes Common.

I interrupted her only once and that was to ask whether she had given any thought to my question about Edith Dearing's ring, but her mood had changed since the previous evening and she replied carelessly:

'I can't remember, but I don't imagine she was wearing it. She hardly ever did when she was alone. Anyway, I don't see what difference it makes.'

And then off she went again, in full spate, about all those things she could remember.

However, there were so many repetitions and irrelevancies mixed up with them that the effort of concentration needed for sorting the wheat from the chaff, while keeping half my mind and both my eyes fixed on the road, quite wore me out. The Bricklayers' Arms had never looked more inviting when, an hour and a half after leaving London, I pulled into the tiny parking place in front of the saloon bar.

This was not the pub on the edge of the village, beside the Common, which was a much superior place, patronised by the local nobs, but was situated about half a mile further up the road towards Dedley and attracted a distinctly more raffish and uninhibited clientele. It was also noisy and not particularly clean, but luckily there was a scruffy garden at the back and side of the house, with one or two rickety wooden benches and tables, and I told Beverly to instal herself at one of them while I went inside to order the drinks.

'Has Jimmie Peacock been in this morning?' I asked the landlord, having purchased a tomato juice and a gin and tonic.

'Not yet. 'Speck he'll be over dinner time, though. Usually manages to get away for a bit then.'

'Don't tell me he's working?'

'Well, no, couldn't call it that exactly. Doing a job for his old lady. Painting her kitchen, or something. Did you want to see him?'

'It's not important. I just thought, if he was around, I might ask him to take a look at my car. The engine seems to be making a sort of banging noise and I've always heard he has rather a way with cars.'

'You could say that, I suppose,' the landlord remarked, looking with an affectionate expression at the glass he was wiping, as though sharing a private joke with it. 'Well, getting on for ten to, so I don't suppose he'll be long now. Want me to carry those out for you, or can you manage?'

'No, with any luck I'll manage splendidly, thanks.'

Beverly was seated under a tree in a chair facing the lane, so I asked her if she'd mind moving over and letting me sit there instead, as I had left my sunglasses in the car.

'That's straight tomato juice,' I added. 'Is that right, or did you mean a Bloody Mary?'

'No, this is just fine. I do occasionally have vodka in it and then most often I wish I hadn't. I get a funny reaction from alcohol.'

'Most people do, from time to time.'

'I know that, Tessa, but mine's different. I get this awful depression. As though something terrible was about to happen to me and nothing in the world I could do to stop it. It must be the medication they gave me when I was sick. They warned me about it at the time, but they didn't tell me it would go on like that for my entire life.'

'I see no reason why it should. From what you were telling me in the car it's plain that you had good cause to feel frightened and depressed. Naturally, you were tempted to try a stiff drink to help you out of it and, naturally, it had the opposite effect. What beats me is why you suffered in silence.

175

Well, perhaps silence is not quite the right word, but making all the wrong noises. Surely you could have confided in Lorraine?'

'No, I couldn't. She gets so panicky about even tiny things and then she has to spill it all out. Sooner or later she'd have told Virginia, however much she promised not to, and then what? I'd be certified insane and they'd shut me up, maybe for my whole life, in that terrible prison I was in before they moved me to Bella Vista. Worst of all was that it might have been true.'

'What might?'

'That I really was crazy. Imagining I'd been seeing things which never happened outside my imagination. That's why I would take a drink once in a while. Only it never worked. It just made me feel worse.'

'Yes,' I agreed, 'it was very cruel and wicked. Unfortunately, though, I doubt if it actually constitutes breaking any law. Unless, of course, you could prove that your health had been seriously affected, which is probably the last thing you'd wish to have proven. However,' I added, as I saw a figure approaching down the lane, 'perhaps we can do better than that. Stay where you are, I'll be back in a minute. Oh, and one more thing, Beverly, don't remove that camera from around your neck. It may be needed.'

He was a bun-faced young man, aged about thirty, with honest blue eyes and a very sweet smile. He looked like a cherub in jeans, an image which he had no doubt cultivated as a boy soprano in the church choir and which had stood him in good stead ever since in his pursuit of acquiring an adequate income without ever doing a stroke of work.

I explained about the problem of the car and, in between cluck-clucking, while peering down into the engine, unscrewing various knobs and screwing them back on again, he described his sadness at seeing his poor old mother, who had toiled away all her life, now so lonely and crippled and how thankful he was to be able to do a few jobs for her around the house.

When this subject was exhausted he closed the bonnet and said that without a doubt it was the transformer valve, or something equally meaningless, that was causing the trouble, adding that he would be only too pleased to help me out, but that it would take him an hour or two to make a decent job of it.

'OK, Jimmie, I'll leave it outside on the Common. I shan't be going back to London before six, so come round any time.'

'Will do, Mrs Price, you can rely on me, and don't forget to leave the keys in, will you? I'll need to give it a test run when I've finished.'

'Yes, of course,' I agreed, wondering what crafty plan had floated into his head which necessitated borrowing my car for a couple of hours. 'Have you time for a drink?'

'Well, that's very kind of you, Mrs Price and I appreciate it. Don't I wish there were more people around here as thoughtful as you are, and Mr Crichton too, of course. It'll have to be a very quick one, though,' he added, recollecting himself, 'otherwise my old mum will be wondering where I've got to.'

He really was quite nauseating sometimes.

Incapable as ever of sitting still for two minutes, Beverly was standing about ten feet away when we reached the garden gate. She had her back to us, her hair glinting like a ball of fire in the full sunlight, and appeared to be taking a photograph of a tree-trunk. Hearing the latch click, she swivelled round and pointed the lens in our direction.

I heard a choking noise beside me and saw that Jimmie had retreated a few paces and was bending over, with his face buried in a handkerchief.

'Are you all right, Jimmie?'

'Yes ... thanks ... ever so much,' he croaked between splutters of self-induced coughing and continuing to stumble away as he spoke.

'That sounds like a nasty cough,' I remarked, keeping pace with him. 'Have you seen Dr Macintosh about it?'

'No ... Mum's always ... on at me, but I ... know what that

177

would mean. ... X-rays, hospital, the lot, most likely,' he replied, beginning to speak more coherently now that we had rounded the corner of the building and were out of sight of the garden.

'All the more reason to see him before things get to that stage. I'd make an appointment right away, if I were you.'

'Thanks, Mrs Price, it's ever so kind of you, but I've got this stuff the chemist gave me and it does help to ease the pain in my chest. I'll nip off home now and take a dose of that.'

And nip he did, with a burst of speed which would have been remarkable in a man not suffering from a serious chest complaint, and I walked thoughtfully back to the garden.

'OK, Beverly,' I said. 'Mission accomplished and we now move on to Toby's. It's nearly time for lunch and the only rule worth remembering in that household is not to keep Mrs Parkes waiting.'

21

'A unique combination, in my experience,' I said later that day. 'No less than three separate criminals and four victims. They overlapped from time to time and, to make it still more complicated, one of the principal victims was also one of the criminals. I only mention it,' I added, 'to explain why it took me over three weeks to unravel all the threads.'

'I am rather sorry you did mention it,' Toby remarked. 'It sounds ominously like sitting here for another three weeks, listening to you ravelling them all up again.'

'My advice,' Robin said, 'which should have a familiar ring by now, is to start at the beginning.'

It was then seven o'clock and the three of us were alone at Roakes, Lorraine having obligingly sent Basil down to collect Beverly, who was replaced an hour or two later by Robin.

'It starts a good way back,' I warned them. 'At least six months before the Mystery Readers' Tour turned up in our midst.'

'For which we have Barbara Landauer to thank, I take it?'

'Yes, indeed. She was the beginning.'

At this point I paused for fully half a minute and Toby said:

'So, after all, we seem to be getting off lightly. It was much shorter than I had dared to expect.'

'That can't really be all you mean to tell us?' Robin asked.

'No, but in striving to follow your advice, I find myself in a dilemma. Although the story begins in the past, logically speaking we should now take a giant step forward to something that occurred as recently as yesterday, when I had my job interview with Mr Ginsberg. Such a lovely man he was, too. I shall feel quite sad when I have to turn him down.'

'Stick to the point,' Robin said. 'That is the second rule.'

'On the other hand, Robin, if you will take some advice from the older man, you will let her get on with it in her own way. Otherwise, this will end by being one of those summits where the protagonists use up all the allotted time arguing about the agenda.'

'Oh, very well. Go ahead, Tessa, and do your worst.'

'It was from Mr Ginsberg that I learned that Barbara Landauer was playing a devious game, whereby she accepted money to collect certain information and, having done so, used the information to blackmail someone else. And that reminded me of something. Edith Dearing and I once discussed a hypothetical crime novel based on some of the characters in the Mystery Tour and she put forward the idea of blackmail being the most likely motive. She was only half serious, but she was a pro, after all, so I listened and began to think about ways to tie it in, if I were writing it. Furthermore, she threw out one or two other theories while we were on the subject and one of them struck me as so startling, and yet so obvious, that I decided to follow it up.'

'I suppose I do tend to be interested in something both startling and obvious,' Toby admitted, 'so you may tell me what it was.'

'Her explanation for the curious relationship between the Neilsens. I'd already begun to suspect that they weren't married, but Edith took it further. Her idea was that Cornelius was the blot on the escutcheon of some rich family who would go to vast expense to hush up his indiscretions. Elaborating on that theme, she came up with the idea that there was some almighty scandal blowing up, involving a young girl, and they had hustled him out of the country until it blew over. Well, that seemed to hang together. Lorraine had already told me that the Canadian in the party had found Cornelius's attentions to his daughter objectionable and, of course, we all know what a dead set he made at Beverly. Not that she was ever in real danger from him. Her heart was already pledged elsewhere, but that's another story.'

'And, if you ask me,' Toby said, 'I can't see that this one does much to prove that he and Mrs Neilsen were not married.'

'Ah, but you see, Edith had worked it all out. She said that since he obviously could not be let loose on his own in some foreign country, the family had hired someone reliable and discreet, in other words a professional, to tag along and keep him in order.'

'Very ingenious, but fiction nonetheless.'

'Not altogether, Toby, because, remembering a remark of Beverly's, I backed a hunch. I sent a message to Henry, asking if he could dig out some information concerning a Mrs Helen Neilsen and suggesting that a good place to start might be in the mental home where Beverly was incarcerated at the beginning of her breakdown and which she was so terrified of being sent back to. Yesterday evening Lorraine telephoned with the news that someone of that name had recently been employed there as a part-time nurse. How about that?'

'Amazing! What a triumph for you!'

'A double one in a sense, because, as well as showing how shrewd and observant Edith was, perhaps too much so for her own good, it also proved that Beverly was not suffering from delusions about everyone she met being someone she had met before. It was quite natural, when she remembered where she had first seen Mrs Neilsen, to conclude that she was being kept under observation. As a matter of fact, she had nothing to worry about there either. It was someone else, who, for reasons of his own, was going flat out to convince everyone that she was mentally unstable.'

'And who could that have been, I wonder?'

'I bet you've guessed already, Toby, but just in case you're not humouring me, I shall keep you in suspense for a moment or two while I sweep another small matter aside. I refer now to Mervyn.'

181

'I am all for that. I have been waiting to do it for years, but I should not have had the temerity to dismiss him as a small matter.'

'Insofar as that, although his role is that of second victim, it had only a remote connection with Barbara Landauer's murder.'

'So someone was blackmailing him?' Robin asked, and Toby said:

'I trust they took a packet off him? I doubt it, though, since I imagine this is where Jimmie Peacock enters the story?'

'You're right. He was out and about near the Common, as is his wont on a fine Sunday afternoon, on the lookout for unconsidered trifles and he found a real beauty when Beverly left her camera on the ground and went dandelion-hunting. I expect he'd noticed her right away. With all that orange hair glinting in the sunshine, she would have been hard to miss, although I daresay he was even more struck by the gold chain glinting round her neck. So when she obligingly put it within his grasp, she must have appeared to him as an apparition from heaven. All he had to do was scoop it up and hare off home, there to remain until the pawnbroker opened his doors on Monday morning. Naturally, he would have taken the precaution of mentioning to his mother that, if anyone should come round asking questions, she was to remember that he had not left the cottage during the whole of Sunday.'

'Yes, I can see all that,' Robin said, 'but where does the blackmail come in?'

'Ah well, the foregoing only applies to the gold chain. Before disposing of the camera, he had to get rid of the half-used film inside it and it's fair to assume that he was not certain of being able to do that without damaging the camera. So, waste not want not being the motto, what more practical than to use up the rest of it, call in at the photography shop, get them to take the film out and leave it there to be developed and printed, before flogging the camera? It wasn't until he had been back to collect the prints that he realised what a goldmine had fallen

182

into his hands. Good old Beverly who, as we all know, took as much care over photographing a chair-leg as the sun rising over Mont Blanc, had recorded several scenes on the Common and in the lane which separates it from the wood. In the car coming down today she admitted that one or two of them had contained views of people and cars, both passing and parked by the roadside. It is not hard to guess who one of them represented and why Jimmie thought his lucky star was burning so extra bright.'

'I can hardly believe,' Robin said, 'that you have proof that he thought anything of the kind, still less that he had been blackmailing Mervyn.'

'I don't need proof. That's for Sergeant Matthews to worry about, if he thinks it's worth his while. My point is that it's the only logical way to account for Mervyn's distaste for the subject of Mrs Landauer and also Jimmie's sudden excess of funds. I don't suggest that either of them had any hand in the murder, but if Mervyn had taken the long way home, after dropping the Professor off at the station, in order to delay his return until she had left, and if this could be shown to have happened, he might have had some explaining to do with the police. And nothing will persuade me that it wasn't Jimmie who stole Beverly's camera. He damn nearly fainted when he saw the copy she was wearing this morning and he couldn't wait to get away before she recognised him. Not even the prospect of turning a dishonest tenner and making free with my car for a couple of hours could detain him.'

'All the same, if he had offered to sell Mervyn the incriminating photograph, which I take to be your premise, I can't see Mervyn tumbling into that trap. What was to prevent Jimmie having half a dozen copies made and selling one off every time the funds ran out?'

'His own limited mentality, mainly. He could never have kept up a long-term operation of that kind without losing his nerve. His policy has always been to grab what's going and then get out, and no one knew that better than Mervyn.'

'Right. So now you think you've disposed of that, how far do we have to go leaping back for the next bit?'

'Well, it does pre-date what has gone before, I admit, but only by a few months and Mervyn is once more in the spotlight. The scene has moved to New York and he is dining in some posh restaurant with Mr Ginsberg of the High and Wide Travel Bureau, with whom he has just concluded a mutually satisfactory deal. Mervyn, as you'll recall, is about to go into the tourist business on a grand scale by hiring out his shoot to parties of rich Americans, and they were working out dates and details for the forthcoming season. Also having dinner at this restaurant, which is probably why it had been chosen, is Barbara Landauer.'

'Did this Ginsberg really let you into all these secrets?' Toby asked.

'Not in so many words, but he did tell me that at about this time he had hired Barbara to do a special undercover job for him, which in fact consisted of spying on one of his business associates, and he also made it plain that he did not then sit back and leave her a clear field, but kept tabs on everything she did. We don't need to suppose that he told Mervyn this, but enough must have been said or hinted for Mervyn to take a good look at the man she was dining with.'

'Why must it?'

'Because he recognised him again when he turned up in Oxford last week. And there, I have to confess, I did him a grave injustice. It is nice to know that I was able to make amends so promptly by spiking the guns of that skunk, Jimmie Peacock.'

'I should have been in no hurry myself,' Toby said. 'What is this new side to Mervyn which makes it possible to do him an injustice?'

'I imagine she feels a twinge of remorse for having worked so hard to get a murder charge laid at his door.'

'Worse than that, Robin. The truth is that when he warned me against Colin Gascoine, I automatically interpreted it as a

184

threat, but I was wrong. It was a warning, pure and simple.'

'When did he warn you against Colin Gascoine?'

'Oh, you remember! He and his ma came round to my dressing room after the performance and when they'd left he made some feeble excuse to come back. Colin had the seat next to his in the stalls and Mervyn must have recognised him straight away as the man who had been dining in New York with Barbara Landauer, whose nefarious activities were being scrutinised by the president of the High and Wide Travel Bureau. Colin recognised Mervyn too, you can be sure of that. It was what drove him to make his gallant offer to switch places with Lorraine.'

The narrative had to be interrupted here to explain to Toby who Colin Gascoine was and afterwards Robin said doubtfully:

'I thought you were rather pro-Colin and everyone I met spoke of him in such glowing terms. What sort of nefarious activities are you accusing him of?'

'At first, I went all out for blackmail, with Edith in mind. Of all the characters in my imaginary reconstruction, he was the one who was most ideally placed for a bit of that. You know, finding out shameful secrets about some of the clients and blackmailing them after they got home. However, at some point during yesterday evening's events, I realised that everything would hang together twice as neatly if he were the one who was being blackmailed. The question was, what for?'

'No good asking me,' Toby said.

'The most plausible answer was theft. He was equally well placed for that and it would have been twenty times simpler to carry out. I don't mean theft on a systematic scale, just one quite good haul every so often, when the conditions were just right. I imagine, too, that the method would have been similar in each case. For instance, he would have waited until the very end of the tour before going into action. By that time he'd have sorted out the very rich from the not so rich and, having whittled the first group down to the most promising few, or even a single individual, would have learned as much as

185

possible about what valuables they had brought with them, where they were normally kept and so forth. It would also have had the advantage that on the last day, with all the confusion of packing and leave-taking, buying last-minute presents and all the rest of it, there was a reasonable chance that the victim might not discover that some valuable item was missing from its case. Afterwards he or she would doubtless have been in correspondence with the hotel about it, but when nothing resulted from that it's unlikely that they'd have complained to the travel agency and of course they had no means of comparing notes with people who had been on other tours. Nevertheless, there must have been one or two occasions when something of the kind did happen. Enough, anyway, to alert Mr Ginsberg and eventually he came up with a common denominator in such cases as were reported.'

'And called in Barbara Landauer to investigate it, I suppose?' Robin said.

'Quite right, only unfortunately she cheated and turned it to her own advantage. He's a lovely old thing, Mr Ginsberg, and a very astute businessman, I feel sure, but perhaps not the world's foremost judge of character. Providing her with information of that kind was like handing her rubies and pearls. All she had to do was to tell Colin what she knew, without naming the source, and offer to refrain from passing it on to his employers and the Director of Public Prosecutions in return for a slice of the profits.'

'Supposing for the moment you were right, and before you get down to the murder itself, how did Beverly fit into all this? Was she collaborator or victim?'

'Oh, victim all the way and through no fault of her own, poor girl. If anyone was to blame, it was Lorraine and I for allowing her to wander off on her own for half an hour because that's where it all began.'

'And a ghost called Colin walked on the Common?'

'It does make sense. You remember how wildly excited she had been up till then? It was only afterwards, when she came

186

back clutching the dandelions, that the mood had changed. Lorraine said that on the drive down she had behaved like someone who was drunk on champagne, or had fallen in love for the very first time. Both, she added, being equally improbable, but she was wrong there. Beverly had fallen in love, although not with Cornelius, as everyone supposed, but with Colin.'

'She admitted it?'

'Confirmed it for me, you might say. It was probably inevitable. He was very personable, with loads of charm when he chose to exert it, and he lived and prospered by being all things to all men. That's why, having recognised Edith as an observant, well-informed woman, as well as rich, he singled her out for special treatment, laying himself out to supply her with interesting details about the places they visited. And I daresay it was the work of a moment to assess Marilou as the downtrodden poor relation, stuffing herself with rich food to compensate for her arid life and very likely resenting the arrogant, demanding aunt who was regarded by everyone else as such a sweet old lady. I am sure it was just Colin's automatic knowledge-is-power reaction to everyone he met, but it probably came in handy when he needed to drop a few hints as to who might have had the neat idea of wedging the sweet old lady in the lift doors.

'Lorraine, of course, was a very different cup of tea and, to start with, he made a dead set at her. It didn't last, though. As soon as he discovered, as would have happened within the first half-hour, that instead of the rich and unattached widow of his dreams, she was the wife of an eminent New York lawyer, he changed his tune and moved on to other prey.'

'But where was the advantage of persuading a girl like Beverly to fall in love with him?'

'Purely an automatic response, as I said and, in her case, it must have been irresistible, wouldn't you say? Even someone a lot less experienced would have grasped in two seconds that she was all set to kick over the traces and so starved of affection that she was ready to fall in love with the first man on offer, particularly one so much older than herself.'

'The good old father-figure touch?'

'I'm afraid so, and it wasn't only Earl's death which had created this void in her life. She'd always yearned to be Daddy's own special baby girl and she tried to kid herself, and me too, that she had been. It was a myth, though. Lorraine made it quite plain that Virginia was the one he'd always doted on and then, just as she was about to embark on married life and leave the field clear for Beverly, naughty old Dad had to go and drop dead. It was all nicely set up for Colin, but his attitude soon changed. Within forty-eight hours Beverly had become his most hated enemy.'

'And so back to the ghost, at last?'

'Yes, Beverly has admitted she saw him, or someone awfully like him, when she was searching for her camera. She told Lorraine he was packing luggage into the boot of a car. That would have been a picnic box, obviously. He would have taken great care to ensure that he was not seen lunching in public with Barbara Landauer.'

'And he saw Beverly watching him?'

'Shouldn't think so. He'd have been in no mood for casting eyes over the landscape. His mind would have been fixed on getting out of that place, as fast and as far away as was humanly possible before the body was found. In any case, he didn't need to see her. She told me that he'd said something about spending Sunday in the country, but he'd named some place on the coast. She was so vulnerable that even a silly lie like that made her uneasy and, although she vowed not to tackle him about it, she couldn't hold out for long. I daresay it all came pouring out on that very first evening they spent together, when she claimed to have been invited to go to the cinema with the Neilsens. He denied it, of course, and teased her about seeing his face in every star, or some such rubbish, but from that moment on she never stood a chance. Colin set about systematically doing everything in his power to undermine her confidence and ruin

188

her reputation, both mentally and morally. I daresay there was vindictiveness in it, too, but the main object was to ensure her being accepted, even by those closest to her, as a hysterical, thieving little tramp, whose word counted for nothing. All this, of course, to forestall any accusations she might make against him in the future. Hence the shoplifting charade and hence also the planting of the yellow string glove, so like the pair Cornelius had bought in the same shop. Of course, he knew he was safe to go into that bedroom without compromising himself. He made it his business to know exactly what was going on and he was not such a fool as to drop the pretence, with her, of being her ardent admirer. Even to the extent of replacing the poor darling's lost camera, although omitting, naturally, to mention that the gold chain was a fake. And by keeping in close touch with her throughout the Cambridge jaunt, he also knew that she and Lorraine would be staying at the New Westminster. Why else would you and I have had that carefully contrived accidental meeting with him in the Arena Bar? He knew perfectly well that we should be arriving at the hotel at seven o'clock and anyone who'd made any sort of study of Lorraine could have banked on her keeping us waiting for at least ten minutes. He never had any intention of coming to see me in Oxford. It was simply a device to strengthen his alibi. Didn't it strike you as strange, Robin, that someone who, on his own admission, hadn't even found the time to unpack should be padding around looking for chance acquaintances in a place like the New Westminster?'

'I did notice that he seemed curiously unsurprised to find us there, but I attributed that to a different cause.'

I saw Toby's eyebrows go up at this point, so said quickly:

'No, we were just stooges, a small part of the main strategy.'

'What strategy?'

'Pinching Edith Dearing's diamond ring, of course. What else?'

'Oh, did he do that too? Wrenched it off her finger and marched out, so causing her to drop dead with a heart attack?'

'I don't imagine he would have been quite as crude as that. It's more likely that he'd have walked in, the door being unlocked as usual for Marilou, and picked the ring up from the bathroom. I don't know whether the idea of setting up the bottles and glasses was a last-minute improvisation. I daresay, though, that when Edith's cry of alarm was followed by total silence, he would have taken a chance on her being unconscious at least and, finding it to be so, went to work to put another nail in Beverly's coffin. He'd already added to the smokescreen around his own movements by passing on a phoney message to her from Edith. I admit that I can't be exactly sure of the details, but I daresay Sergeant Matthews will be able to get them from Colin, if he feels inclined to try and if he ever catches up with him, which I now begin to doubt.'

'Personally, I don't forsee much trouble there, if it should be necessary,' Robin said. 'He told you he was on his way home to his wife and we know the name of the firm in Canterbury, so they'd have his private address. I think it might be worth giving Matthews a ring, though, before he retires for the night. He may want to come over and talk to you and, if so, he'll probably want to see Beverly as well. Time to think about getting in touch with Colin Gascoine after all that.'

'Not time enough, I fancy.'

'Why? What bee buzzes in that bonnet now?'

'One that hums the refrain that Colin is even now busy with his plans for withdrawal. I have the strong suspicion now that his famous wife and family don't exist. It came to me, much too late unfortunately, that I had completely misinterpreted Mr Ginsberg's reaction to my remarks on that subject. The sad fact is that Colin, intuitive to the end, had probably felt instinctively that things were beginning to close in on him and it was time to stage one final coup and then get out. Acquiring a new passport and a new identity would be all in a day's work to him and I haven't much doubt that, given another twenty-four hours at the most, he'll be halfway across the world and Sergeant Matthews will have missed whichever bus he's travelling on.'

'Well, I suppose nothing's lost by setting a few wheels in motion,' Robin said, getting up in an ostentiously slow movement. 'What was the name of that Gloucester travel agent?'

'Eros.'

'Oh, very appropriate. And I must say, Tessa, I'm rather surprised at your ever hitting on that one as the villain. I had the sort of impression that you found him ... well, rather sympathetic.'

'Goodness me, no,' I said, 'I wasn't fooled for a minute. I daresay I might have fallen for his bogus charm when I was Beverly's age, but I've become more discriminating now. It must have something to do with the company I've kept.'